C.O. JONES

AIRSHIP 27 PRODUCTIONS

C.O. Jones: Mobsters and Monsters
© 2015 Fred Adams Jr.

Published by Airship 27 Productions
www.airship27.com
www.airship27hangar.com

Interior illustrations © 2015 Clayton Hinkle
Cover illustration © 2015 Carl Yonder

Editor: Ron Fortier
Associate Editor: Charles Saunders
Marketing and Promotions Manager: Michael Vance
Production and design by Rob Davis.

ISBN-13: 978-0692483589 (Airship 27)
ISBN-10: 0692483586

Printed in the United States of America

10 9 8 7 6 5 4 3 2 1

C.O. JONES
MOBSTERS AND MONSTERS

BY FRED ADAMS JR.

CHAPTER ONE

Newark, New Jersey, 2 June 1948

Fracturing the human skull in the right spot requires only fifteen pounds of pressure per square inch. The man called Lattimer could have done it with his bare hand but opted to use a sap instead. The object was to take out a thug standing guard without either of them making any noise in the process. Hit him hard, hit him right, and the guy would go out without as much as a grunt.

The guard was nervous, which didn't help Lattimer, but he was a hometown amateur, which did. The guy was leaning against the rough brick of a warehouse wall instead of standing loose and sure-footed. His cigarette dribbled ashes on his double-breasted pinstriped suit as his head jerked from side to side trying to watch every direction at once. The guard's eyes peered from beneath the brim of a dark fedora that made him look like Central Casting sent him for a George Raft movie. His right hand was inside his coat Napoleon-style which let Lattimer know he was carrying under his left arm, probably a small revolver. He was young, early twenties at the outside, and scared to death, which made him a wild card, more dangerous in some ways than a predictable pro.

Lattimer wore dark green chino work pants, steel toed lace-up boots, and a waist-length zip jacket. Except for the slouch hat that hid his face, he looked like any blue collar stiff headed to work as a stevedore or a mechanic.

No rush here, he thought, tucked in a nearby shadow. Just wait until the cigarette burns down and he needs both hands to light another one. The half dozen butts at the guard's feet told Lattimer his assessment was on target.

Somewhere in that warehouse was Bobby Torreo's sixteen-year-old daughter Lilly, snatched, if you'll pardon the pun, from Lover's Lane where she was parked with her date, a foolish kid named James Holdorf. They probably should have gotten a room in some hot pillow joint, but Daddy's little girl couldn't risk being spotted and had to sneak around.

Holdorf apparently tried to defend Lilly's honor with a ball bat he pulled from behind the seat and got two slugs in the head for his trouble.

After an anonymous phone call, Torreo's boys found Lilly's clothes, Lilly's purse, and Lilly's dead boyfriend, but Lilly was gone.

Torreo's men moved the car and threw the body into the river. The romance was a secret, and the kid's parents, who were nobodies, thought James was rolled. The Mary Jane that Torreo's guys spilled under the steering wheel led the cops to write the killing off as a disagreement among hopheads, so they didn't look at it as hard as they might have.

It had been two days and Torreo managed to keep the Newark cops in the dark about Lilly. Then an envelope arrived in the afternoon mail at Torreo's headquarters with a note demanding one hundred grand in cash. When Bobby opened the envelope, a fingernail fell out. Plier marks in Lilly's distinctive shade of nail polish showed Torreo the kidnappers weren't playing around. Instead of calling the cops or calling New York, Torreo called Lattimer.

The guard threw down his butt and crushed it out with the toe of a shiny shoe. Lattimer was right; the right hand came out of the coat to fumble a cigarette out of a deck from his left hand. Lattimer darted from the shadows and by the time the hood realized he was there, Lattimer was already swinging the blackjack. It connected with a crack dulled by the man's hat, and the guard fell without as much as a whimper. Lattimer pulled a snub-nosed .38 from a shoulder rig under the hood's jacket and shoved it into his pocket.

He threw the limp body over his shoulder and carried him to the far side of a car parked nearby. A quick pass with his Ka-Bar slit the back of the man's suit coat, and Lattimer used it hang him in a slouching position from a side mirror so that if anyone looked outside, they would think he was still watching the henhouse.

Three steps and Lattimer was at the entry door. The lock was no problem. A few seconds with the right picks and the door swung inward. Dim light from dusty bulbs showed him what he needed to see. Bales of cotton yarn for the Jersey textile mills were piled ten deep forming a maze of aisles. He pulled his .45 and thumbed back the hammer. Lattimer listened closely. The cotton soaked up sound like a sponge would water, but from the back he heard faint sounds of movement and what sounded like cries of pain.

Lattimer ran as silently as a panther through the maze of cotton bales, at the same time orienting himself for the sprint back out. He slowed as the sounds became more distinct and turned a corner to see two men dressed like their pal outside crouching by a doorway. The men were taking turns peering through the keyhole, and Lattimer realized that the cries he heard were cries of passion, not pain.

Lattimer crept closer. One of the hoods elbowed the other aside, and while he was off balance, Lattimer kicked him in the side of his head, throwing him into his partner. The second hood, caught by surprise put balance ahead of defense and instead of grabbing for his piece put his hand out to catch himself. Amateurs. Lattimer brought the .45 down across the bridge of his nose and on the backhand broke his jaw. In the overhead light, Lattimer saw that they were kids. Neither could have been more than eighteen.

From the other side of the door came a voice: "What the hell are you two doing out there?" Lattimer turned the doorknob. It wasn't locked.

The bare bulb overhead showed the room was small, maybe eight feet by ten, probably an emptied office. A table and two chairs stood against one wall, the table littered with food and bottles. A movie magazine lay open to a photo spread of Jane Russell. The only other furniture in the room was a narrow bed with two naked people under the covers. One of them was Lilly. The other was Benno Benaducci's snotty punk of a son, Eddie.

Lattimer smiled. "Hi, kids. Hate to say it, but playtime's over."

Eddie tried to reach for his trousers hanging on the nearby chair and got tangled in the covers. He fell out of the bed, pulling them off Lilly. She gasped and in a display of fake modesty pulled a pillow over her breasts. The hands that clutched the pillow sported all ten nails. "Oh, thank God you're here! It was terrible! He did awful things to me!" she babbled.

"Save it, honey," said Lattimer. "You aren't fooling me or anybody else. Game's over." Lattimer stepped to the bed and grabbed Lilly by the wrist and hauled her to her feet.

"My old man'll get you!" snarled Eddie.

Lattimer laughed. "If Bobby Torreo doesn't kill you himself, your old man will probably do it for him for putting him in a bind like this. Did you have to shoot that poor dumb kid?"

Lilly started to struggle but couldn't break Lattimer's grip on her arm. She swung her free hand at his face and clawed at his eyes with her red fingernails. Lattimer cracked her on the side of the head with his gun hand and she went limp.

The distraction gave Eddie enough time to lunge for his trousers and come up with a small caliber automatic. The Sight showed Lattimer what was coming and he dodged as Eddie fired, throwing himself between the girl and the gun. He felt the hornet sting of a slug in his shoulder and swung the .45 in Eddie's direction. The pistol boomed like a cannon in the small room. Eddie's head came apart and brains and blood spattered the wall behind him.

Lattimer threw the limp girl over his shoulder and on his way out grabbed a cut glass nail polish bottle from the table and dropped it in his pocket. One of the guys at the door was lying where he left him. The other wasn't. Lattimer didn't wait around to see where he went. He took off at a dead run, the nude girl bouncing on his aching shoulder. A shotgun roared behind him and a bale of cotton exploded near his head, spraying a snowstorm of white fibers. Lattimer wheeled and fired three shots in a spread to span the aisle and drive the young gunman to cover.

Like a ballet dancer, Lattimer finished his turn and took off running again. The shotgun boomed, but no closer; the shooter wasn't chasing him. The kid had learned a big lesson: It's no fun when the target shoots back. Ten seconds and Lattimer was at the door. He yanked it open and nearly stumbled over the outside guard who had come to and fell over the sill when the door opened. Lattimer stepped over him with a foot between his shoulder blades and ran to his parked car.

The old '40 Ford coupe stood at the curb like a faithful horse. Lattimer yanked the passenger door open and threw Lilly on the seat and locked her in. He turned the key and the engine growled. He put the car in gear and pulled smoothly away from the curb; no burning rubber, no attracting undue attention. As Lattimer rolled from streetlight to streetlight, he stole a look at the unconscious Lilly. She was cute, but not exactly to his taste. She'd be a handful for somebody some day and he didn't envy her father the years in between. He pulled a rough blanket from behind the seat and threw it over her, slowing down to twenty-five. He didn't want the cops pulling him over with a naked underager beside him.

It was three a.m. when Lattimer pulled up to the back door of Bobby T's. He cut the headlights and tapped the horn two short, one long. A door opened, throwing an angle of light across the alley and two of Bobby's men came out. Lattimer stepped out of the car hands at shoulder height and empty palms forward. "Lattimer with a delivery for Mr. Torreo."

One of Torreo's boys led Lattimer to the boss's office while the other carried Lilly inside. Torreo's desk and chair dominated the Spartan room. The comfortable guest seat in which Lattimer sat was the only other furniture. The desk was a mass of mahogany waxed to a mirror shine. There was nothing on it but a telephone; no pencils, no pens, no desk blotter, just the phone. Unlike so many restaurateurs, his walls had no autographed celebrity photos, no pictures at all, in fact. When Bobby was in his office, nothing distracted him from you, and nothing distracted you from him except one item.

In one corner a scarred old baseball bat, its handle wrapped with raveled friction tape stood; a reminder of Torreo's youth when he made his stones with the mob and earned his monicker as Louisville Bobby breaking the legs and cracking the skulls of recalcitrant protection "clients" for his father Big Jimmy.

The doctor came in. He was a bent old codger with a gin blossom nose and rheumy eyes. The old man pried a .25 caliber slug out of Lattimer's shoulder as gently as a gravedigger and marveled at the array of scars and tattoos on his torso "I've seen a lot of scars in my time, son," he said, "but never so many in one place." He cleaned the wound with peroxide and swabbed it with iodine that stung worse than the bullet. He was bandaging Lattimer's shoulder when Bobby Torreo came into the room.

He looked to the doctor. "You done?"

The doctor tore a bandage longways and knotted it under Lattimer's armpit field-dressing style. "Yes, sir. Right now." Torreo handed him an envelope. The doctor took it and nodded his thanks to the Boss. "Always a privilege." He backed out of the room and closed the door behind him.

Lattimer was tall, but Torreo was taller. The gangster was dressed at three a.m. as if he were going to lunch at the Ritz; dark suit, white shirt and a red tie with a pearl stickpin. "How did you find her so quickly?"

"The job had amateur written all over it. They didn't cover their tracks very well. And who has steak dinners from Carlton's delivered to some rat-trap warehouse? It was mostly A plus B."

"What tipped you off it was a fake?"

"The nail polish on the fingernail. Where the pliers chipped off the fresh coat of red, there was a different shade, cheap stuff underneath. They probably paid some poor hooker, painted her nails and pulled one out to send to you. When I went through Lilly's purse, all her other stuff was there, lipstick, compact, comb, perfume, but no nail polish. When I searched her room, I didn't find that shade on her dressing table either." He pulled the cut glass bottle from his pocket. "This was in the room where I found her."

Torreo's dark eyes squinted at the bottle as he turned it between his thumb and forefinger. "So she and that little bastard Eddie did this to shake me down." He threw the bottle across the room and his fists clenched in fury. "What did they think they were going to do?" he snarled. "Run away together? Live happy ever after? Didn't they think I'd find them no matter where they went?"

"'Think' is the key word," said Lattimer buttoning his shirt over the bandage. "I guess Eddie and his pals got ideas watching the old man and thought they'd give crime a whirl. Too bad they didn't stick to stealing candy from the corner store. And, Mr. Torreo, I apologize for knocking out Lilly, but we might not have gotten out of there alive otherwise."

Torreo grunted. "You did what you had to do." He reached into his suit coat and pulled out an envelope. He handed it to Lattimer and said, "I have no complaints, but Benno will want your head on a plate for Eddie. It was a righteous kill, Lattimer, but losing his only son . . ." Torreo's voice trailed off.

Lattimer folded the envelope without opening it and put it in his pocket. "I understand."

Torreo opened the door and motioned to someone in the hallway. "I sent two of my boys to your place to collect your belongings." One of Torreo's bodyguards came in carrying Lattimer's battered valise. "I figured Benno would show up there sooner or later once word got around."

Lattimer nodded. "Thank you, Mr. Torreo." Implicit in the mobster's gesture was Torreo's message that it was time for Lattimer to move on— now.

Torreo held out a slip of paper to Lattimer. "A suggestion; you'll have to manage your own introductions."

Lattimer turned it over in his hand. It read: 220 Snowdon Square, Brownsville, Pennsylvania.

CHAPTER TWO

Lattimer had two more stops to make before he left town. He drove his car to the riverfront along rows of darkened warehouses until he reached a dilapidated pier. He cut his lights and rolled to a stop.

The pier was deserted; the only sound was the lapping of the river against the pilings. Lattimer stole across the warped planks along its edge and shinned down the third piling into the dark water. He slid his hand down the post until he found a hook with a thick rope tied to it. Lattimer reeled up a heavy sack and slung it over his good shoulder then climbed back onto the pier. All clear if you didn't count the rats.

A quick drive over the bridge and Lattimer was in Brooklyn. He wound through alleys and back streets until he reached an unmarked garage tucked cheek to jowl between the back ends of two larger buildings. He blew two quick blasts on the horn and in a moment the door rolled back.

A short wiry man in coveralls looked out and waved Lattimer inside. The cavernous interior of the garage belied its outside appearance. Walls had been knocked out of the adjacent buildings, more than tripling the garage's interior space.

Immediately ahead were lift racks, grease pits, work benches and other features common to garages everywhere. A dozen mechanics and shop men labored on cars. The noise of hammering, grinding, and revving engines was deafening. Some cars they were tuning, some they were painting, some they were dismantling, and some they were dismembering with torches. To the right and left of the work area were ranks of every kind of car and truck in the City; sedans, convertibles, delivery vans; even a stolen postal truck and a Brink's armored car.

The little man shut the door and Lattimer got out, hands away from his body. He nodded to a sentry with a sawed off pump shotgun stationed just inside the door. The guard nodded back and Lattimer relaxed. He turned to the little man. "Hello, Speedy. Busy tonight?"

Speedy was short and swarthy, a shock of dark hair spilling from a greasy red leather ball cap. A twisted white scar from a piece of shrapnel at Anzio divided his forehead like a drunken meridian. "Busy every night, Lattimer. We cater to the vampire trade. They don't come out 'til after dark. Whattaya need?"

"As much as I like these wheels, I need them to go away."

Speedy pulled a pack of Camels out of the front pocket of his coveralls and shook out two, giving one to Lattimer. He lit the cigarette, took a drag and dribbled out the smoke from the corner of his mouth. He said over the racket, "That can be done."

"And I need a crate." Lattimer walked around and opened the trunk. "Big enough to hold this bag."

"Leaving town?"

"Leaving the planet."

"Damned shame to cut this baby up. Some of my best work."

"I figured you'd want to save the engine; that's why I brought it here."

Speedy nodded. "Okay. But you're lucky I owe you, Lattimer. I get the feeling somebody's gonna come around asking about you. So what kind of car do you want to replace it?"

"No car, Speedy, just a ride to Grand Central—and the crate." He peeled five one-hundred-dollar bills from his roll and handed them to Speedy, who nodded and tucked them in his pocket. "I'll get you that crate."

"And Speedy—thanks."

Speedy grinned around his cigarette. "We vets gotta stick together."

A half hour later, the man called Lattimer sat on a bench in Grand Central Station. The big clock said 5:20 and except for a few sleeping bums and an old guy pushing a broom, the place was empty. He sat on a bench, reached into his valise, dug under the cheap cardboard bottom, and pulled out a waterproof envelope. In it were three IDs with different names. He flipped through them, found the one he wanted, and put it in his wallet. The old one that said Lattimer went in pieces into three separate trash cans.

He shouldered the crate and went through the portal that led to the freight dock. The dock was busier than the station, men in coveralls rolling hand trucks piled with boxes to one train or another. A tired looking clerk handed him a freight ticket without even looking at him. The man called Lattimer filled out the ticket and handed it back to the clerk: C. O. Jones, c/o Union Station, Brownsville, Pennsylvania.

As the sun rose, the man now called C. O. Jones leaned back in his seat in the passenger car and pulled his hat over his eyes. The train ride to Baltimore would take at least ten hours.

CHAPTER THREE

As he slept, the dream came again. He was a raw recruit on the parade ground at Claiborne in 1942. The new inductee stood at parade rest, one more faceless guy in green on his way to the shooting gallery, head shaved, dressed in fatigues too new to lose their stiffness. He was in the front rank, but if a giant mirror stood opposite them, he would have had to wave his arm to find himself in that anonymous mass. He was known as Simmons then, and there were thousands like him, rank after rank sweating at parade rest in the hot sun and cursing the generals for putting them on review in the Louisiana humidity.

"Atten-hut!" The Sergeant-Major's voice cracked like a drover's whip and the green ranks of his company snapped to attention. A chicken colonel, hands behind his back, strolled almost casually along the ranks like a shopper in a department store browsing merchandise, or a cattle dealer culling a herd. The Colonel's face would have been handsome except for a thick scar that ran across his left cheek to his upper lip. Grey hair showed below the rim of his hat. His khaki uniform was immaculate; rows of decorations on his chest. Beside him a shrunken tattered rat bag of a woman in a rusty black dress and a shawl matched his stride despite her age. She could have been eighty, ninety or a hundred years old, wearing that badge of maturity, the crumpled waxed-paper face of the old Cajuns who lived a world away in the bayous.

A voice from a back rank whispered, "Maybe somebody raped her daughter and stole her pig." Another voice replied, "Or looked at her daughter just raped the pig instead." She stared straight ahead as she passed them, but a few steps past Jones, she put a hand on the Colonel's elbow and they stopped.

The crone turned a pair of dark eyes toward him and the young recruit named Simmons realized that she was blind, but felt that she saw him just the same—not just his face, but everything behind it. She raised a crooked finger and pointed him out. "That one, him," was all she said, with that odd emphatic pronoun that Cajuns affect. The Colonel beckoned to the suddenly special recruit and said simply, "Come along, soldier."

The Colonel's name tag read Hennessy, and he spoke to the Master Sergeant who took Buck Private Simmons to a waiting Jeep. He climbed into the front and the M.P. behind the wheel drove away without a word. The Private didn't ask where they were going or why; he knew the Army would tell him what they wanted to tell him when they wanted to tell him. In ten minutes, the Jeep pulled up to the Command Center and the M.P. led him through a side door into the cool darkness of the building and down a corridor to a room with no name on the door. The walls were bare except for an oblong mirror on the one opposite the entrance. Inside he found a table and a half-dozen chairs but no ashtray.

"Have a seat, soldier."

"Can I smoke?"

"Sorry, pal, not in here. The Colonel doesn't approve of it. Like they say in the Navy, the smoking lamp is off." The M.P. left and for the next hour, Buck Private Simmons stared at the blank walls and his reflection in the mirror. The face that stared back was anxious but not afraid, a distinction without a difference. Finally, he drifted into a fitful doze.

He jerked awake to footsteps in the corridor. The door opened and when Colonel Hennessey strode in, Simmons jumped to attention.

"At ease, Private." Hennessey took a chair at the head of the table. Even in his seat, the Colonel seemed to be at attention. "Sit down, son. Relax. I expect you want to know what's going on here, and I can tell you enough to ease your mind, in some ways, at least." The door opened and an adjutant came in, saluted, handed Hennessey a green cardboard file folder and left. Hennessey opened the folder and without looking up said, "Tell me about yourself."

After hearing a few fumbling minutes of autobiography, Hennessey asked The Question: "Private, have you ever found that you are, shall we say, different from other people or special in some way?"

"I don't understand, sir."

"Do you have any abilities that are apart from those of everyday people?"

Buck private Simmons felt his flesh crawling. "What do you mean, sir?"

Hennessey's hand slapped the table like a pistol shot. He snarled, "Dammit, Private, don't play dumb with me. You're a special case. Madame Lavois knew it, I know it, and you know it." Hennessey's voice softened. "I'm not here to hurt you, son, I'm here to help you use your talent to the fullest extent. Now tell me about it."

Late in his childhood, the soldier known as Simmons realized that he could see how things would turn out, not way ahead of time, but an instant before they happened; no more than a second or two. He'd feel a tingling, not physical, but in his mind. When one of his friends threw a basketball at the hoop, he often knew when it would go through the rim or bounce away and where to run to catch the rebound.

A bully who tried to sucker punch him on the playground one day found himself swinging at empty air and getting a bloody nose in the bargain. Once when he and his friend Davey were hunting rabbits in the woods, Davey stepped over a fallen tree and the boy saw a rattlesnake strike from behind the log and shoved Davey out of the snake's reach before it struck. When he told Grandma about it, she called it simple intuition, but she also cautioned the boy to keep the story to himself.

Another time, years later, when he was accused of cheating in a poker game, a drunken loser pulled a pistol, put it in his face, and pulled the trigger. Before the hammer fell, he saw the chamber was empty and cold cocked the bastard and ran before he could pull the trigger again. He couldn't control the Sight as he came to call it; it came and went unbidden but always proved correct. The Sight was no free ride, either. His head often hurt afterward, sometimes for days, and more than once he wished it would go away.

Hennessey listened to the account without a twitch of an eyebrow or a blink of surprise. Then he said to the mirror, "Bring in a deck of cards, please," and Buck Private Simmons realized the room was wired for sound and people must be watching them through a one-way mirror like the one he'd seen once in a police movie. In a moment, the adjutant brought a new Hoyle poker deck. Hennessey tore off the wrapper and shuffled the cards. "Show me."

As the Colonel turned the top card, before Simmons could see its face, the two of clubs flashed in his mind. "Clubs—two," he blurted.

Hennessey flipped the card face up and nodded. "Again." He started to turn the card and before it was face up Simmons said, "Queen of diamonds."

"Again."

"Eight of clubs."

After a few more successful tries, Hennessey put his finger on the top card but didn't turn it. "What's the card?"

"I don't know, sir. I can't see it."

"Guess."

"Uh—three of hearts?" Hennessey flipped the card and as he did, Simmons saw he was wrong before the face turned up. Six of spades.

Hennessey turned another card. "Nine of Diamonds."

He put a finger on top of the deck. "Next?"

"I can't see it yet. I guess things have to be moving before I can see them, sir."

"I'll be damned. Maybe the power is kinetic." Hennessey jotted a note in the file, collected the cards and absently tapped the deck on the table, thinking. Finally he looked up and said, "I've read your file, Private. No next of kin?"

"No, sir. My parents were killed in an auto accident. My grandmother raised me until she died, and then I went to an orphanage. I was adopted when I was fourteen, but my stepfather must have thought he adopted a mule the way he worked me on his farm and beat me. I ran away and joined a carnival when I was fifteen and never went back."

"No wife or children?"

"No, sir."

"No fiancée or girlfriend who'll come looking for you?"

"No, Colonel."

"Private Simmons, you are in a unique position to serve your country in its time of need. What I will now tell you is highly classified and to be held in the strictest confidence. Do you understand me?"

"Yes, sir. I understand."

"Have you ever heard of the Office of Strategic Services, the O.S.S.?"

Buck Private Simmons had heard barracks talk about the elite cadre of operatives—call them what they were—spies who were trained in some secret camp to go behind enemy lines to gather intelligence. Their clandestine nature led to a mythology of almost superhuman proportions including spectacular tales of assassination, demolition and glamorous adventure. "A little, sir, but not much."

"I can tell you that I command one such unit, a special one within the Service. We have known for a long time that Hitler is preoccupied with the occult and the supernatural. We have recently learned that the Nazis are scouring Europe and the world for that matter for objects and people with supernatural powers to use as weapons against us. We need people with special talents to counter that force, and you are apparently one of them. Congratulations, son. You're about to be promoted."

"Sir, I don't think I…"

"Don't think, Private. Just say yes." Hennessey reached under the table and pulled up a .45 automatic. He aimed it at Simmons's forehead. "After what I've told you, national security demands that if you refuse, you don't leave this room alive." He cocked the hammer. His finger tightened on the trigger. "One, two…"

The tingle. Buck Private Simmons saw the live round in the chamber and his sense of survival overrode his judgment. "Yes, sir. I'm in."

Hennessey thumbed down the hammer on the .45 and lowered the pistol. "Welcome to the O.S.S., Lieutenant Simmons."

Jones woke to the conductor's call for the Penn Station in Baltimore. Two days later, after taking a second train to Wheeling, West Virginia and a third to Pittsburgh, he was done reading *War and Peace*. Time to find another book.

CHAPTER FOUR

The old rummy doctor stared at the bottle. He'd been staring at it for forty-five minutes. Benno Benaducci sat across the table in shirtsleeves, his tie pulled down. He poured three fingers of gin from it into a glass. "You know what I want, Doc, just tell me."

"I can't, I . . ." His voice trailed off.

Benno turned his hands palm up in a mock gesture of supplication. "A name, Doc, just a name. You patched up some hitter at Bobby Torreo's place a couple of nights ago. Just tell me who he is." Benno picked up the glass and waved it under the old man's nose.

The doctor drooled at the tantalizing scent of the booze. "I don't know his name. Nobody ever said."

"Okay, so you did patch somebody up." Benno's dark eyes narrowed.

"Now we're getting somewhere. So tell me, Doc, this no-name, what did he look like?"

"He was tall, dark hair, a body like Tarzan. Scars and tattoos. I've never seen so many tattoos."

Benno swirled the gin in the tumbler. "Like what? Anchors? Names? Betty Grable?"

"No. Greek letters, and circles and triangles and such with lines through them, words in Latin, and other stuff I didn't recognize. They were all over him"

"And the scars?"

"Gunshot wounds, a couple of knife wounds, even a chunk bitten out of his side. Most of them looked as if he sewed them up himself, like maybe in a fox hole."

Benno pushed a pencil and paper across the table. "Draw me a picture."

The doctor drew a crude human shape and embellished it with lines and figures. When he was finished, he turned it around for Benno to see. He studied it for a moment then held it up for his men. "Ring a bell?"

All shook their heads. Benno pushed the gin across the table, and the doctor grabbed the glass with both hands, choking on the cheap booze as he gulped it down. Doc put the glass on the table and as he reached for the bottle, Benno nodded to one of his men who put a bullet behind the old man's ear.

Benno stared at the spreading pool of blood from the dead man lying face down on the table. It wasn't enough revenge for his son, not nearly enough. But it was a start.

CHAPTER FIVE

Brownsville was a town that had long passed its zenith, but it was still a long way from its sunset. Founded in Colonial times, it boasted the first cast iron bridge in the United States, built in 1839 to accommodate the National Road (later U.S. Route 40) and still bearing traffic. Located along the Monongahela River, the intersection of the National Pike and the River made it so prosperous that in the early days of the Republic, people believed that Pittsburgh wouldn't amount to much because it was too close to Brownsville. A hub for the coal and coke business, the town thrived in the twenties to the point that on Saturday nights, the business district was closed to auto traffic because the throngs of pedestrians spilled off the sidewalks and filled the brick streets.

In the thirties when the coal ran out, Frick, Carnegie, Thompson and their counterparts picked up the money and left the area lying along the railroad tracks like an empty purse and stranded a whole generation of transplanted immigrants in the middle of the Depression. The Pennsylvania river towns reflected that era.

Jones was awake for the whole rattling train ride from Pittsburgh to Brownsville and marveled at the similarity of the towns that lined the Monongahela River. It was as if he were not on a train following a linear path but on a merry-go-round turning him to view the same repeated scene. An eerie similarity exists among most Mon Valley towns; river on the left, paralleled by railroad tracks, a few business district streets, then to the right, enclaves of houses embedded into steep hillsides rising sharply from the valley. At one end of town lay its principal business, a mine, coke ovens, or a steel mill. The other end trailed off into increasing desolation and clusters of ramshackle houses.

The scene reminded Jones of a piece he'd read once by H. L. Mencken that described a train journey through Western Pennsylvania. Mencken described the view from the train window as "a scene so dreadfully hideous, so intolerably bleak and forlorn that it reduced the whole aspiration of man to a macabre and depressing joke." Jones, having traveled through a good part of the world had to agree. Here were Mencken's "dingy clapboard houses . . . set upon thin, preposterous brick piers. By the hundreds and thousands these abominable houses cover the bare hillsides, like gravestones in some gigantic and decaying cemetery." Not the most likely place for a new start, thought Jones, but opportunity is what you make of it.

The train pulled into Brownsville at 7:00 a.m. Jones stepped off and the first thing he noticed was a pair of men walking out of the Red Feather Tavern across the road. In fact several of the bars he passed along Front Street were open and busy. In a world of rotating shifts and twenty-four hour operation, the bars, diners, and brothels had a twenty-four hour clientele.

Food first. Jones followed a side street along the railroad tracks that led him under the Intercounty Bridge where he found a diner called Fiddle's; checkerboard tile on the floor and milk glass globes that hung by chains from the ceiling. The pedestal stools along the counter were filled with men in work clothes; railroad workers from the roundhouse, laborers black and white, weary from a shift of pulling coke from the beehive ovens that proliferated like mushrooms along the railroad tracks, and welders and fitters from the Hillman Barge Works. They were either tired and grimy from coming off a shift or relatively clean and ready to go at it again.

Jones slid into an empty booth and set his valise on the floor by his feet. A dark-haired waitress in a snood and a clean but threadbare uniform with "Ellie" stitched on the breast scurried over with an order pad. "What would you like?"

Jones ordered ham and eggs with hash browns and coffee. For forty cents, it was a decent meal. Any town that served a good working man's breakfast that cheap couldn't be all bad. While he ate, Jones picked up snatches of the conversation from the counter. He heard six opinions on the Pittsburgh Pirates' chances for a pennant this season, what Truman should do with Korea – and China while he was at it, and what number to play that night.

When Ellie brought his check, Jones asked her where he could find a room. "The Brownsville Hotel up the hill has the best rooms and the fewest cockroaches," she said with a laugh. "Or if you're on the cheap, try the Manson near the railway station. Or if you want a boarding house…"

Jones shook his head. "That's all right. I'll try one of the hotels. Thanks." He left her a dime for a tip and as he walked out, he said to the room in general, "Any of you know who's hiring right now?"

One of the men at the counter said over his shoulder, "The rail yard always needs shovel men at the coal dock, if you don't mind back breaking work. Ask for Bob Hankins."

"Thanks for the tip. Shall I tell him you sent me?"

The man laughed. "Hell, no. I just quit the job three days ago." The others joined in and Jones did too. He picked up his valise and stepped out into a bright morning.

The town was waking up and starting to bustle. Store owners were rolling down their striped canvas awnings and sweeping the sidewalks. Traffic was already filling Market Street. The cars and trucks were mostly pre-war, but occasionally a new Caddy or Mercury or Buick would roll by, a sign that the town and the area were still prosperous. Maybe it wasn't the twenties anymore, but the town boasted three movie theaters, a bowling alley, two five-and-dimes, and its own daily newspaper.

A kid was hawking the papers to drivers stopped at the traffic light. Jones waved him over. "*Telegraph*, mister, or *Herald*?"

"Both." Jones handed the kid a fifty-cent piece and said, "Keep it." The

"What would you like?"

kid grinned and turned back to the street. As the boy pocketed the coin, Jones saw the steel platform of a leg brace showing below his trouser cuff. "Thanks, mister," he said, limping away.

"Hey, kid," said Jones, "which way is Snowdon Square?"

"Right around that corner, two blocks," he shot over his shoulder as he scuttled around to the driver's side of a red Packard sedan.

Jones jaywalked through the traffic and in five minutes he was sitting on a slat bench across the street from 220 Snowdon Square. The building shared the block with a grocery, a shoe repair shop, the Post Office, and a ladies' clothing store. 220 Snowdon Square was four stories high, old brick with some fancy terra cotta trimming around the tall windows, probably built during the coal boom of the nineties. The first floor sported big paned windows with the word Pool in gold leaf. The window shades were down on the first floor but some of the second floor windows were open and from above, Jones heard the unmistakable tattoo of gloves on a speed bag. There were four empty parking spaces in a row in front of 220 and down the street, but nobody pulled into any of them. Drivers passed them by for spaces further away in front of other shops and storefronts.

He lit a cigarette and opened the first of the newspapers, *The Brownsville Telegraph*. Time to learn about the new turf. He had finished reading the *Telegraph* and was halfway through the *Morning Herald* from Uniontown, the county seat when the cars started pulling into the empty spaces. The first was a new Cadillac, black and shining like polished onyx in the morning sun. A second car pulled in right behind, a big Buick, dark blue with tinted windows. The driver doors of the Caddy and the Buick opened and men in suits got out. Big guys. Bad guys. They walked around their respective cars and opened the passenger doors.

A man in a brown suit with a loud necktie got out of the Cadillac and limped to the door of the poolroom. Jones had been around enough vets in the hospitals to spot a fake leg at a hundred yards. The driver opened the door of the Buick and a short man in a hundred dollar pinstripe suit and a dark fedora stepped into the street. He nodded to the bodyguard and walked around the front of the car. The man was short, but he looked perfectly proportioned and he moved with a fluid, athletic grace.

The short man unlocked the door to 220 and they all went inside. In a minute, the shades went up. 220 Snowdon Square was open for business. In the next hour, two more cars, both of them expensive and shiny parked in front of 220, and men in expensive and shiny shoes got out of them and went inside.

The last car to pull in was a brand-new Mercury convertible, baby blue with what had to be a custom made white rag top. The driver got out and Jones saw a stocky man dressed in pegged pants and a white shirt, no tie, a cigarette dangling from his lip. His dark hair was long and slicked back, and his face was the image of the short man's. Brothers.

From his vantage point on the bench, Jones could see into the poolroom. He watched for a little while longer. Nobody was shooting pool. Nothing was moving. He stood up, folded the newspapers under his arm, picked up his valise, and started up the hill toward the Brownsville Hotel.

The room wasn't bad at all, especially compared to some of the places Jones had flopped in Jersey. Room 307's window gave a nice view of the brick wall across the alley; the bath was at one end of the hall and a window with the fire escape outside it was at the other just a few feet from Jones's window. The mattress was a lumpy cotton tick, the sheets were changed three times a week, and a light fixture missing its glass cover offered a bare bulb as the only light in the room. A single chair and a low dresser completed the furnishings. Jones paid a week in advance, three dollars and fifty cents, put his valise under the bed, and stretched out for a nap. Nothing of interest would happen in Brownsville before the sun went down.

CHAPTER SIX

After a fifty cent steak at Fiddle's Jones sat on the same bench he had earlier and enjoyed a cigarette while he watched people come and go through 220's door. It was seven o'clock at night and the same four cars were parked in the same four spaces. People came in suits, people came in work clothes, and people came in uniforms. Some of them stayed a while, but most were in and out in a few minutes. Half the pool tables were busy, and upstairs, the sounds of the boxing gym were multiplied. Lights were on and the ceiling-high windows of the second floor gave him a view of a ring, hanging bags and sweaty men working out. They lifted weights, skipped rope, and shadow boxed along the walls. He also caught a glimpse of a walled off stairway to the third floor.

As the sun set, lights glowed through the blinds of the third and fourth floor windows, but Jones couldn't see what lay behind them. There must be the real action. He ground out his smoke and crossed the street to the door. Everything stopped for a few seconds as Jones stepped inside while every pair of eyes took his measure. Back in the far corner at a table a little better kept than the other eight, the dandy from the blue Merc was shooting a game with the short man, now in his vest and shirtsleeves with his tie still knotted at his throat. The pair studied him for a moment then went back to their game. As if that were a signal, so did all the other players.

220 Snowdon Square looked, sounded and smelled like any poolroom Jones had ever been around. The oiled oak floor was old, its grain pushing up like corduroy whales and digging into his soles. Shaded lights hung low over the tables and put the upper half of the room in shadow. Tall platform chairs lined one wall as if the Supreme Court would be judging the matches. The guy with the fake leg sat in the one closest to the counter, his trouser cuff riding high enough to show a dull aluminum shin over the top of his sock. A blue haze of cigarette and cigar smoke hung in the air, and the crack of the balls was augmented by the sounds of the fighters upstairs.

Jones stepped up to the counter and a lean buck-toothed guy in suspenders and a striped shirt turned away from the cue he was repairing. His eyes had a bright look to them that said "booze" and the teeth gave him a misleading look of amusement. "You here to shoot, Bud?" he said, "Five cents a rack."

Jones smiled without opening his mouth. "No, I want to know about upstairs." Bucky's eyes twitched and Jones saw his hand reach under the counter. "The gym; I want to work out in the gym."

Buck-teeth let out a breath and by the smell; Jones knew he was right about the booze. "Be right back." He went to the back table corner and said something quiet to the short man who nodded and turned back to sink two balls on a three cushion shot before he stepped away from the table. He walked over to Jones and held out his hand to shake. "I'm Skitch Mottolla. I own the place." He waved a hand at the guy with the fake leg. "That's my partner Jack Mozzo." Jack raised a hand in acknowledgement. "They call me Jackie the Leg," he said with a laugh, rapping on his metal shin."

"So," said Skitch, "What can I do for you?" Although it was evening Skitch was perfectly tonsured and manicured and despite the blue cast of a heavy beard looked as if he'd just been shaved by a barber.

"I'm C. O. Jones." He shook hands with Skitch. Despite his size, Mottolla's grip was firm and his hand was hard as a rail spike. His build was compact and Jones judged he'd be a handful in a street fight. "I'm new in town," Jones said. "I saw your gym through the windows and I'd like to make some arrangement to work out there."

Skitch stepped back and eyed him up and down. "You a pro?"

Jones shook his head. "Nope. Boxed in the Army. I fought light heavyweight in the ring a few times since; nothing big-time, but I like to stay in shape in case an opportunity comes up."

Skitch nodded and said over his shoulder, "Hey, Bucky, set this man up with a locker." Then back to Jones, "You shoot pool?"

"A little."

"Come in early for your workout sometime and maybe we'll play a few games."

"Come on, Skitch," yelled the Merc man. "Table's getting cold."

Skitch grinned. "Excuse me. My brother Dodie gets impatient when he's losing."

Jones decided Skitch's affable persona was his most valuable asset.

Bucky tapped Jones on the shoulder. He held out a tarnished brass key. "Locker 27. That'll be fifty cents for the week, in advance."

Jones handed him a dollar bill. "Let's go for two weeks to start." Bucky threw the bill into the cash drawer under the counter. "See you tomorrow," said Jones. He nodded to Bucky and headed for the door, feeling every eye in the place on his back. Brownsville was an interesting town.

CHAPTER SEVEN

The next morning, Jones went back to Fiddle's. Ellie set his ham and eggs in front of him. "Find a room?" Jones smiled. "Yeah, at the Brownsville Hotel." He laughed. "They gave me the presidential suite. Thanks for the tip."

Ellie grinned. "That's how you earn them," and before he could respond to her quip, she hustled back to the service window to pick up an order. When Ellie came back to top off Jones's coffee, he asked her. "Since you know all about Brownsville, where can I get my laundry done?"

"Try Lee Hing. He's about two blocks from your hotel on Fifth. Anything else you need?"

He grinned, "No, I'm not very complicated." Ellie picked up his plate and as she turned, she said, "Mister, if I've learned one thing working here, it's that everybody's complicated."

Two cups of coffee later, Jones left the diner and strolled to the roundhouse. Bob Hankins was easy to find. He had the loudest and the foulest mouth, cussing every worker and piece of equipment in the place.

Hankins hired Jones on the spot, handed him a number five shovel, a sledge hammer and a worry bar and sent him down to the coal dock. The coal dock consisted of three levels of tracks, the highest sixteen feet above the second. On the second level a large hopper ran on rails perpendicular to the other two. Coal cars stopped on the upper track and Jones knocked their traps open from below with the sledge. The coal ran into the hopper that then dumped the load to the lowest level into the coal tender of one of the dozens of locomotives the roundhouse served every day. The work was a brutal and dangerous ten hours for five bucks a day. Any coal that fell to the side had to be scooped with the clamshell shovel and thrown over the six-foot rim of the hopper. If the traps stuck, muscle and the worry bar came into play. And watch out for the moving cars.

An hour into the day, Jones dripped sweat. Two hours in and his shoulders ached. The job was a bitch, but it was cover for the moment, and a good workout in the bargain. At four o'clock he walked past Hankins. "Coming back tomorrow, Jones?"

Jones smiled. "As long as you pay me."

On his way back to the hotel, Jones stopped in Carter's; a workingman's clothing store and bought a pair of canvas gym shoes and a set of grey cotton sweat pants and pullover shirt. Better to look like he belonged in the gym than attract more attention than a stranger normally would. The bed looked tempting, but Jones strolled down the hill from the hotel to Snowdon Square. He passed through the poolroom with a nod to Jackie. Skitch and his brother were nowhere to be seen. He climbed the stairs and stepped into a familiar world of muscle, leather, and sweat.

The gym was a high-ceilinged room with windows that reached from bottom to top. Most of them were open in the evening heat and Jones wondered whether anyone ever fell through one. The ring was regulation size and well-maintained, as was all the other equipment. Whoever ran the place took it seriously. Men worked speed bags and heavy bags, and a small crowd cheered and jeered as two men sparred in padded gloves and headgear.

Over in a back corner, he saw two men in suits who didn't look like gym rats. One was the driver for Skitch's car, and the other a bigger side of beef. They slouched on either side of an elevator cage.

Jones picked up a skip rope and went to work while he waited for a bag. A minute into the workout, two guys in trunks, gloves, and headgear stepped into the ring and everyone stopped what they were doing and gathered around to watch. Skitch and his brother came out of the elevator and joined the crowd, so Jones put down the rope and stood ringside to watch the two welterweights spar. They were both young and both in good shape, but the boy with the shock of dark hair sticking out of his headgear was a yard past his partner.

"Kid's good ain't he?" said a short, stocky man beside Jones. He had a crooked smile, hair like a handful of dry grass, and a Marine Corps emblem tattooed on his forearm. "Yeah," said Jones. "Real good. Who is he?"

"Name's Tommy Cimino. Skitch is backing him. He fights welterweight; has a matchup with Jack Rodgers in a couple of weeks. The winner gets a shot at Sugar Ray for the title," he said around a toothpick, still watching the fighters.

"And the short-haired kid?"

"That's Bobby Jalso. He's not bad, but he's nowhere close to Cimino."

In the ring, Jalso put up a game fight, but Cimino was just too quick. Jalso barely got a glove on him. The gang around the ring yelled approval every time Cimino landed a good punch. In the far corner, a short, heavy man with jowls like pork chops and a shock of snowy hair yelled directions. His thick arms flailed the air punctuating his shouts.

"That's Fats Mungo, Cimino's manager. He yells at Tommy like he's a dog in a flower bed, but he loves the kid like he was his own son. That's Cimino's wife Roseanne over there, away from the ring." A petite blonde woman in a blue dress, obviously pregnant, watched with a hand to her mouth. "She's always worried about Tommy when he fights, but more now than ever since Ezzard Charles killed Sam Baroudi back in February."

But no one was going to die that night. After five rounds, the fighters gave each other a friendly pat of the gloves and swung through the ropes to the gym floor.

As Jones turned to walk away, the blonde man caught his elbow. "New in town?"

Jones figured the guy was sent over to sound him out. He turned back and held out his hand. "Yeah. Name's C. O. Jones."

"Danny Hayes. What's the C. O. stand for?"

Jones grinned. "Conscientious Objector."

Hayes laughed. "Yeah, I bet. I would've guessed Commanding Officer. You look about as peaceful as a .50 caliber machine gun." He held up his tattooed forearm. "Birdie on the ball here. How about you? What branch?"

"Army Air Corps. Tigers over Rangoon."

Hayes nodded. "If you say so, pal, but I got to say you don't look like a wing washer to me." He shrugged. "But a vet's a vet. You got a job yet?"

"Down at the rail yard on the coal dock."

Hayes grimaced. "That's not a job, man, that's slavery."

"It'll feed me until something better comes along."

"I'll keep my ears open. There's always something new around here. You box?"

"I have, but not lately."

"There's always outdoor pick up fights for some quick bucks if you know the right people."

Jones shook his head. "I stay away from those. Somebody always loses money and takes it out on the winner. Too many people out there with guns; I got shot at enough in China."

Hayes chuckled. "Yeah, you've been around, all right. Well, if I hear of any opportunities, I'll let you know."

"Thanks." Jones looked across the floor and saw two men walking away from a heavy bag. "I'm going to grab that bag while I can. Good talking to you."

"Yes, sir." Hayes gave him a half-assed salute and walked away. Jones watched him go around the corner and down the stairs. Now the locals knew as much about him as he wanted them to—nothing.

For a half hour Jones pounded the bag and felt every eye in the place on him. Around the time he was done, Jones saw the elevator come down and Skitch step out with two other guys in suits. He looked away and concentrated on the bag as the mobsters crossed the gym and headed for the stairs. He looked toward the ceiling. Up there was the real action. Soon.

CHAPTER EIGHT

For the next week except for Sunday, Jones worked the coal dock. Hankins sent three different men down to work with him. Two left after one day and the third after a day and a half. The mindless shovel labor didn't bother Jones much; it gave him time to think and plan. He needed a car, and he needed to deal with the crate still waiting for him at the freight depot. He went to the gym in the evenings and let them see the same face night after night. Before too long he was accepted as part of the crowd.

His second week at the gym Jones stopped his workout to watch Cimino spar again. There was no doubt Tommy had the stuff and deserved the title shot. Hayes sidled over halfway through. "Kid's looking good. He'll fight Jack Rodgers in two weeks."

Fats was unlacing Cimino's gloves when two men in suits stepped through the arch from the stairwell. The taller one was as rough looking as the shorter was polished. The tall one was bald with a fringe of dark hair over his ears and thick scarring like a valance over his eyes. He'd taken plenty of punches in his career. He headed across the floor toward Cimino. The short guy wore a better suit, better shoes, and a diamond ring on his left pinky that Jones could peg all the way across the gym.

"Who are those two?" said Jones.

"The short guy's Mickey Malone, a big-time bookie. The goon with him is Tony Motsko. Motsko was a heavyweight who got kicked out of boxing for taking one dive too many. Now he's a leg breaker for Malone. He's a mean son of a bitch."

Malone hung back while Motsko arrogantly swaggered across the room toward Cimino and Roseanne. Motsko grinned and said loud enough for everyone to hear him, "So, Tommy boy, you gonna name the kid after you, or his real daddy—me?" Like switching off a light, every sound stopped.

Anger flashed in Cimino's eyes and he snarled, "You can't talk to me like that."

"Whaddya think you can do about it? You're out of your league, little boy." Motsko leered. Cimino's hands clenched.

"Oh, hell," said Hayes and ran for the stairs.

Jones suddenly understood what was happening. Motsko, who was a good thirty pounds heavier and had a few inches' reach on Cimino wanted to goad the kid into a fight and hurt him to keep him from winning against Rodgers. Malone would bet against him and clean up.

Motsko sneered. "Why don't you just step in the ring and we'll settle this right now?" He looked over to the wide-eyed Roseanne. "And then after I show your little broad how a real man fights, I'll show her how a real man loves."

Cimino got a wild look in his eyes and drew back a fist. Fats caught his arm and pulled him back. "No, Tommy!" He stepped between them and snarled at Motsko, poking a finger in his chest, "You get the hell out of here you Polack bastard!"

Motsko grinned. "You're gonna put that little punk in the ring with Rodgers? You'll be lucky if he even shows up for the weigh-in. He's a chickenshit coward, and he just proved it to everybody here."

Jones saw his opportunity. He shouted at Motsko, "Hey asshole, you want a fight, try me. I'll bet money you don't walk out of that ring under your own steam."

Motsko blinked and turned to Jones. "Who the hell are you?"

"The guy who's gonna kick your sorry ass, that is unless you're a chickenshit coward yourself."

Motsko, caught off guard, flicked his eyes to Malone. Malone looked Jones up and down and nodded. "I'll take that bet. I have a grand here says Motsko puts you down for good." He held up a thick wad of bills. "Can you take that action?"

Jones nodded. "I have the cash but not with me." At that moment Skitch and Dodie came running in with a half dozen of the guys from the poolroom. Jones turned to Skitch and said, "I'm good for it. Will you stake me?"

In a half second Skitch understood what was up. Jackie the Leg had made it up the stairs by this time and Skitch waved him over. Skitch said something in Jackie's ear and he pulled up the cuff of his brown suit pants. Jackie opened a panel in the side of his hollow leg and handed a sheaf of bills to Skitch who fanned them between his thumb and forefinger. "It's covered," then quietly to Jones, "Don't lose if you can't pay up." He looked Jones in the eye. "We understand each other?"

"Yes, sir," said Jones. "Completely."

Motsko pulled off his coat and tie and climbed into the ring. Unbuttoning his shirt, he said, "We don't need gloves do we, pal?"

"Shouldn't make any difference." Jones ducked between the ropes. His eyes flicked to Motsko's shoes. They were shined to a mirror gloss, but they were unmistakably steel toed, something to watch out for. Motsko was overweight, but that didn't mean he was slow; he had a belly on him but his arms were thick and his chest was broad.

Jones smiled. "Somebody ring the bell."

"I don't need no bell." Motsko stepped forward and swung a haymaker right at Jones's head, but the Sight showed it to Jones first and he ducked under it and came up with a right jab that put Motsko's teeth through his lower lip. Motsko swung an elbow that caught Jones on the shoulder like a hammer. Jones danced out of reach, his left arm numbing from the blow.

Blood ran down Motsko's chin and dripped onto his hairy chest, but he didn't flinch. The goon was a lot tougher than he looked and Jones wondered for a second why Motsko threw fights he could easily have won. Motsko's foot lashed out at Jones's groin and Jones twisted away, catching the heel of Motsko's shoe on his thigh. As he turned, Motsko drove a hard right between Jones's shoulder blades and put him on the canvas. The Sight flashed. Jones saw the thug's size thirteen shoe coming down and rolled away before it fractured his skull. As he crabbed to the side, Jones's foot lashed out and caught Motsko's knee. It didn't break, but he roared in pain.

Jones sprang to his feet and the pair circled each other for a moment. A glint of light showed Jones the piece of steel rod curled up in Motsko's right fist. One more thing to watch out for.

They danced around each other for a moment, bobbing left and right, looking for an opening. Motsko tried another kick. Jones sidestepped it and caught the foot with both hands. He wrenched it hard to the side. Motsko roared again. If the ankle wasn't broken, it was badly sprained.

"I'm gonna kill you, you son of a bitch!" Tony shouted over the cheering of the ringside mob that grew bigger by the minute as people ran upstairs from the poolroom and even from the sidewalk outside to watch the battle.

Motsko fired a hard right at Jones's jaw, but Jones's head flicked away just in time for the loaded fist to swish past his face. The swing put Motsko off balance because of his ankle and the big man stumbled. Jones waded in and drove a hard combination to his kidneys. Motsko would be pissing blood for a week. Time to end this.

Motsko waded in swinging and Jones slipped a punch. As it went wide, Jones's right hand shot under Motsko's arm and his flat fist drove up Motsko's sternum and caught him square in the throat, crushing his windpipe.

Motsko made a gurgling sound and dropped the steel. It rolled away and off the canvas unnoticed. The thug rocked back and forth on his feet for a few seconds, his eyes wild and his arms flailing in panic. He began to turn blue. Jones didn't want him dead, so he had to put him down, and quickly. He threw three hard combinations, left-right, hammering the big man's jaw. Motsko stumbled backward into the ropes but wouldn't go down. Finally Jones threw a hard left that caught Motsko on the tip of his chin as he hooked a leg behind Motsko's knee and the gangster went over sideways. As he fell, he clutched at Jones's shirt and tore it away, revealing his scarred and tattooed torso.

Motsko crashed to the canvas and before anyone could even think about getting into the ring, Jones pulled his Case knife from the pocket of his sweats and slashed across the bodyguard's throat. Pink froth bubbled from the hole. Jones stuck his fingers in it and shouted, "Give me a pipe, a piece of hose, anything." One of the men at ringside caught on and threw his Kaywoodie into the ring. Jones snapped off the stem and shoved it into the makeshift tracheotomy. Motsko's breath came in ragged gurgling gasps.

"Give me some help here," Jones shouted. "Call an ambulance." For a few seconds, nobody moved. They were transfixed by Jones's scars and tattoos. Then as if on an unspoken command everyone moved at once and swarmed into the ring except one lean man in a green suit who moved the other way toward the stairs, out the front door, and down the block to a phone booth.

Green suit pulled a scrap of paper from his wallet and dialed for the Operator. "Yeah," he said and rattled off a number. He drummed his fingers anxiously on the side of the phone, waiting, waiting. "Yeah, let me talk to Benno. This is Squires. Believe me; he'll want to hear what I have to say."

CHAPTER NINE

Jones climbed through the ropes and grabbed a shirt from a ringside table to cover his torso. He also scooped up the steel bar from the floor and walked up to Malone. Turning it in his fingers, he said. "I think you owe me money, Malone."

Malone reached into his coat and snarled, "I'll give you what I owe you, you bastard." Malone froze when he felt the barrel of Dodie's snub-nosed .38 in his right ear. Dodie grinned. "When that hand comes out, Mickey, it better have money in it and nothing else." Dodie cocked the hammer to punctuate the sentence.

Malone pulled a sheaf of bills from his pocket and laid it in Dodie's outstretched palm. "Time to go home, Mickey," Dodie said. The bookie glared at Dodie and then at Jones. "This isn't over, pal."

Jones stared him down. "It's never over, Malone. It's never over."

Malone turned and shouted at Skitch, "I'll be back!"

Skitch pulled a roll of bills the size of a baseball from his pocket. "Bring your money, Mickey." He threw the wad into the ring. "I'm betting on Jones."

Ten minutes later, dressed in his street clothes, Jones stood with Skitch and Dodie and watched as ambulance attendants lugged a stretcher full of Motsko down the steps. Danny came up behind him and said, "Remind me to never piss you off."

Outside, the siren faded as the ambulance roared up the hill to the hospital. Skitch handed Jones the money. Jones fanned the bills and said, "You backed me. Take out whatever you think is right."

Skitch shook his head. "No, it's all yours, Jones. I don't know you well enough to do business with you yet. You earned every dime, and you did me a favor besides keeping Tommy out of it. Maybe Motsko wouldn't have hurt him. Then again, maybe he would have put him out of commission for keeps. It's a moot point now." He paused, looking over at Dodie as if deciding whether to say it. "And we didn't have to shoot him."

Jones nodded. "How much trouble am I in with the cops?"

Skitch shook his head. "I'll tell you something you may not know. The way the law reads in Pennsylvania, if the District Attorney doesn't bring an indictment, a case never goes to trial. The D.A.'s on our team. Hell, I've been arrested over a hundred times and I haven't seen a courtroom yet. You see that big guy in the blue suit standing by the ring? That's Willie Lang the County Detective. He'll take care of the cops. They don't much care for Motsko anyway. Malone may be another story. Watch your back."

He was almost at the stairs when Skitch called to him. "Hey, Jones, exactly what did you do in the war?"

Jones turned and smiled. "Army Air Corps."

"That's where you learned all that?"

"Battlefield triage—if we got shot down over enemy territory, they weren't sending any medics after us. We had to handle our own."

Skitch shook his head. "That wasn't what I meant." He rubbed his lower lip on his teeth, thinking, then looked up and said, "Go on. We'll talk again."

Jones touched his hat with two fingers and headed down the stairs. He walked through the poolroom to calls of "good fight" and "way to go" and out into the night. On the sidewalk he passed Cimino, his wife and Mungo. Mungo nodded a greeting. Cimino gave him a look that mixed gratitude with resentment. He was three steps away when Roseanne ran after him and caught his arm. "Thank you," she said hardly louder than a stage whisper. Jones smiled and said. "A thousand bucks is thanks enough, Ma'am. Besides, I never did like bullies."

He was halfway to the hotel, when he heard footsteps on the sidewalk behind him: three men. "Hey, buddy," one of them called out. Jones turned and saw the thugs silhouetted against a neon sign. "Hand over your money and you won't get hurt." The speaker, the man on the left, had a pistol in his hand pointed at the ground.

Jones reached into his pocket and curled his fingers around Motsko's steel. He didn't expect to need it so soon. "You boys made a mistake."

They looked at each other and laughed. "Mistake?"

"You let me see which one of you has the gun. Remember, you started this." Jones twisted and whipped the steel bar overhand. It hit the gun man square between the eyes and he went down. The pistol clattered on the sidewalk and before his friends could grab it, Jones closed the distance and dropped the second one with a hard left to the side of his head. The third pulled a knife and slashed at Jones, who put his left forearm out parallel to his chest and the ground and circled so that he was silhouetted instead of his attacker. His Case knife would take too long to pull out and open; better to do this bare-handed.

After a few unsuccessful swipes, the knife man stepped in and tried to thrust his blade like a fencing foil. Jones met him head on, twisting to the side away from the blade. He caught the man's arm under his own and heaved his weight around, bending the attacker's elbow the wrong direction and breaking it with a sharp snap. The knife fell to the bricks and its owner fell to his knees beside it. The knife man screamed. Jones kicked him in the face. He quit screaming.

None of the three moved on the sidewalk. In fact, nothing moved on the whole street. If anyone saw the fight or heard it, he wasn't having any of it himself. Jones picked up the pistol. It was rusty, its grips wrapped in friction tape. It may not have even fired. Jones shoved it into the waistband of his trousers. These meatheads were independent operators; they probably didn't even know how much he was carrying. If they were from Malone, they'd have all had guns and the guns would all be decent ordnance.

Yep, Brownsville was an interesting town.

CHAPTER TEN

The next morning Jones passed the newsboy on his way to the diner. He bought a *Telegraph* and as he tucked it under his arm, he said, "What's your name, kid?" The newsboy raised a suspicious eyebrow. "It's okay, pal; I'm not going to hurt you. I want to hire you to do something for me."

"What's that?"

"I'm going to give you some money, and on your way down here every day I want you to shove a copy of the *Telegraph* under the door of room 307 at the Brownsville Hotel." Jones held out a ten-dollar bill. "You keep half for yourself. When the other half is used up, leave me a note with the paper and I'll give you more cash."

"...Jones....dropped the second one..."

The kid took the bill and stared at it then looked up at Jones and grinned. "Sure, mister. I'll start tomorrow."

"Okay, kid. One more thing: when you put the paper under the door, put it through headline down." Jones grinned. "I don't like to read bad news before I'm ready."

Jones started walking away and the kid called after him, "Thanks, mister. And my name's Marty. Joe Hunnicutt's my dad."

Jones nodded. "Good to meet you, Marty. My name is C. O. Jones."

Marty blinked. "You? You're C. O. Jones? The guy who planted Tony Motsko?"

Jones smiled. "Don't forget my paper." Word got around fast in a small town.

He read the *Telegraph* over breakfast. There was no mention of Motsko or the three muggers. Apparently in a town like Brownsville, like so many that size things that happened after sundown didn't make the next day's paper. A day later, they weren't worth the ink. Time to go to work.

The brutal labor on the coal dock served two purposes for Jones. First, it put him in shape equal to the best times of his life. Second, it gave him a legitimate identity in Brownsville. Nobody thought too hard about a guy who worked for five bucks a day and slept in a cheap hotel. If he'd blown into town living high with no job anyone could see, he'd attract the wrong kind of attention. All he wanted at this point was to get close to the boys at 220 Snowdon.

His fight with Motsko had made an impression on plenty of people. It won him some friends and made him some enemies. Cimino owed him big. The title fight with Rodgers was close, and if Motsko had busted the kid up, Cimino may have healed, but he would have gone into the ring gun-shy and lost the bout for sure. He hated Jones for stepping in and taking away his chance to prove himself against the bully, but in his heart, once he cooled off, Cimino knew how it would have turned out.

Skitch owed him too. The boss hated to admit it, but it was true. Giving Jones the whole bet was a way of passing off his obligation. The fight was Jones's introduction. Where it led was a coin still spinning in the air. Jones just had to wait until it landed one face up or the other.

Skitch had plenty of muscle guys, no doubt about that, and from what Jones could see and hear they were good enough. They ran the town, but even they had some rules to follow. Sooner or later something would come up that put a toe over the line and Jones figured Skitch would know who to call. In the meantime, Jones was housed, clothed, and fed. What else was there? As for Mickey Malone, the bookie was a coward, and his bull dog Motsko wouldn't be busting any heads for a while.

The whole town heard about the fight and the prize money by the next day. Jones was free to spend a little now that he didn't have to explain its source. Time to look for a car.

That night in the gym, Jones strolled up to Hayes while he was working the speed bag. He'd been at it a while. His thatch of blonde hair was matted with sweat to his forehead. "You got a car, Danny?" Jones said.

"Sure," Hayes replied over the tattoo of the bag. "It ain't much, but it runs. Need a ride someplace?"

"Wondered if I might rent it for a day. Got a little business I need to take care of."

Danny let the bag die down. "Do I go to jail if the cops run the plate?"

Jones laughed. "Hell no, nothing like that. Just need to go see some people. How's twenty bucks sound?"

Hayes nodded. "Sounds like you rented yourself a car. When do you want to pick it up?"

"I don't work Saturday, so how about I take it Friday after work, and I'll bring it back the next day, if that's okay with you."

"Sure, just so you have it back for me after supper." He grinned. "Got a heavy date."

"Good enough."

Hayes nodded and as he turned back to the bag, Jones said, "Maybe you can tell me. Who runs the most successful moonshine operation around here?"

CHAPTER ELEVEN

The local consensus was that the moonshiners the Feds wanted to nail more than anyone were the Lytle brothers, Bud and Grover. Mountain boys at the east end of the County, the Lytles were the most prolific, the most successful and the most elusive. Every revenue agent in the tri-state area included their downfall in his prayers at night. Jones figured, and rightly so, they were also the most dangerous; his kind of people. A little more asking got him a location, a back road gin mill too far from civilization to belong to any town. It didn't have a name, just a sputtering orange neon sign that said "Beer." Word was if he was looking for the Lytle brothers, he'd be most likely to find them there.

On Friday he cleaned up after work and met Danny at the poolroom. Danny's car was a green Pontiac sedan that looked as if the running boards might fall off if he slammed the door too hard. The rust flecked paint hadn't seen wax and a rag for years. But when Jones turned the key, the engine came alive and when he stepped on the gas, he realized that the shabby exterior of the car was camouflage for a high powered machine.

He handed Danny a twenty through the window. "I'll get everything done I need and have it back for you this time tomorrow," Jones said, adjusting the mirror. As he drove off, he reminded himself that nothing in Brownsville was quite what it seemed to be.

Jones took Route 40 east through Uniontown to the mountains. The Pontiac took the mountain with ease, and Jones enjoyed the scenery. The Chestnut Ridge of the Allegheny Mountain range was the backbone of Appalachia. The trees were early summer green and made the mountains look like a rumpled carpet in the late day sun. He topped the ridge, passing the Mount Summit Inn, a big, white Victorian resort hotel and caught himself wondering what it would be like to spend a week there with fine food, a bar with top-shelf stock, maid service, and clean sheets every day. Someday, maybe, just not now; not that he couldn't afford it.

The directions he got from an old coot at a gas pump in Chalk Hill sent him off the National Pike into the dense pines of the Allegheny forest. As he turned from one road onto another, each was worse than the last; ruts, mud, and rocks between the tire tracks that threatened to tear off the Pontiac's oil pan.

Nearly three miles into the mountain forest, Jones saw the sign: Beer. The evening came early in the thick pines and Jones's headlights were on when he pulled into the gravel parking lot. The building was clapboard with a long slope to its corrugated roof. A few faded tin signs for Fort Pitt Beer and Chesterfields were tacked up along a porch lined with empty chairs that spanned the front of the place.

The parking lot looked like a junkyard. Rusted rattletrap pickup trucks and battered pre-war sedans lined the lot with one exception: a gleaming Mercury two-door sat at the far end with a rangy man in jeans and a flannel shirt leaning against it. The hayseed eyed Jones with professional scrutiny. A cigarette dangled from his right hand and he cradled a 12-gauge pump in the crook of his left arm. Jones knew he'd come to the right place.

This was the kind of bar that rough people frequent because they aren't welcome anywhere else. Jones had seen plenty of them in place after place; dives and juke joints full of bad people who knew each other and respected each other's space but could erupt in violence at the wrong word, gesture, or look. He felt every eye in the room follow him from the door to the bar. Across a sawdust covered dance floor a gaudy jukebox blared Hank Williams's "Hey, Good Lookin" and a cloud of cigarette smoke hung in the air like Frisco fog.

The bar stools were pedestals bolted to the floor, probably so they couldn't be swung or thrown in a fight. Jones sat on a cracked red leather seat at the end of the bar near the pool cue rack, just in case. The crowd was mostly men dressed in overalls and work-shirts, denim, chambray, and flannel. He faced the bar and watched them in the mirror from under his hat brim. A few heads tilted together and one of the men, a big one with his sleeves torn off at the shoulders stood up. Jones figured the sleeves were missing to show off arms the size of most men's thighs, corded with muscle and sinew. An anchor tattoo with "USN" on his left bicep and the name Cecil on his right forearm read Jones the man's pedigree. A pair of dark piggy eyes glowered from beneath his boulder of a forehead. Jones watched in the mirror as the forehead turned to the right and nodded, acknowledging an unspoken cue.

The bartender, a stout man with a bald head and a grey mustache brought Jones's beer about the time the hulking hillbilly stepped up behind him. The bartender smiled, took Jones's quarter and sidled down the bar away from what was coming.

"What the hell you doing here, city boy?" Cecil's voice was surprisingly high and nasal, cutting through the jukebox. His breath smelled of beer and harder alcohol.

Jones braced his left foot against the bar rail and took a long pull from his beer before answering. "I'm looking for the Lytle Brothers, Bud and Grover. I heard I'd be likely to find them here," he said to the face in the mirror.

Cecil put his big hands on the bar and Jones read his knuckles. More scars on the left hand than the right. He'd most likely lead with his left, and at the moment from a tactical perspective he was on the wrong side of Jones. He was pretty drunk too, which was another point in Jones's favor. "What if they don't want to be found?"

"Then I suppose I won't find them." Jones eye flicked to the others in the mirror. No one moved. They were all watching the show.

"You're a real smart ass, city boy."

Jones set his bottle on the bar and said to Cecil's reflection, "Better that than a dumb ass like you."

Cecil's hands left the bar. He grabbed Jones's jacket but before he could haul him off the stool and throw him to the floor, Jones swiveled and in a move worthy of Harry Houdini, slipped out of the jacket's sleeves and spun to the left, leaving Cecil holding the empty coat and looking like a stupefied toreador.

Cecil dropped the jacket. He hauled back his left fist and Jones danced just outside his roundhouse swing. Jones ducked under the arm and stepped in to push his fingers into the notch of bone just above Cecil's sternum. He didn't punch Cecil, but instead pushed off from the bar, like a sprinter from the starting block, driving the choking hillbilly backward across the dance floor where he slipped in the sawdust and went down hard on his back. Cecil tried to sit up but a good hook to his jaw with a fist wrapped around a roll of quarters put him back down and out.

Jones looked around the room. No one moved. He picked up his jacket, shook off the sawdust and walked back to his stool and his beer. No one got up to drag Cecil away. No one breathed. Jones was finishing his bottle when the bartender came to him and said, "You wanted to see Bud and Grover Lytle?" Jones nodded once, never taking his eyes off the crowd in the mirror. Apparently he'd passed the test. Anyone who couldn't get past Cecil wasn't worth the Lytle brothers' time. "Come with me." The bartender came around the bar and gestured for Jones to follow him. He led him to a door next to the jukebox and opened it. "In here."

The backroom was small, about ten by ten with a low ceiling following the slope of the building's tin roof. Beer cases were stacked high against one wall. There were no windows or other doors, and Jones noted that a single naked bulb overhead was all the light in the room, useful to know if he needed sudden darkness.

A scarred square table sat in the middle. On it were a few beer bottles, a few glasses, and a half-empty Mason jar of what was likely moonshine. Behind it two men were sitting, hands on the table. They looked enough alike to be twins if one of them didn't have a few strands of grey hair to tag him as the older of the two. If not bookends, salt and pepper shakers.

Dark-haired, dark-eyed, and rawboned, the Lytle brothers looked what would pass for handsome in back country, big chins, straight noses, and deep blue eyes. The one to the right wore a bright yellow shirt with tiny blue birds embroidered on the pocket. The one to the left wore a robin's egg blue shirt with short sleeves and a string tie that sported a star on its clasp. Both wore their hair in a pompadour style Jones had seen on the *pachuchos* and the zoot-suiters in Los Angeles and wondered which one of them brought it home from the war.

The bartender brought a chair in and left, closing the door behind him.

Jones pulled the chair up to the table and sat, making himself the apex of a triangle dead center between the brothers. No one spoke for a moment. The bass of the jukebox thumped through the wall but there was no other sound. Jones mirrored them, hands flat on the table. No weapons, no threat. The older brother, the one in the yellow shirt, finished his cigarette and ground it out on the table top. When he wasn't smoking, his lip curled up showing a row of perfect upper teeth. "Maybe you'd like to tell us who you are and what you want with us," he said without so much as moving his head.

Yellow shirt's voice had a nasal twang to it that made it sound as if he were whining and sneering at the same time. The pair stared at Jones more with curiosity than anything else. He smiled and turned his hands palm up.

"My name is C. O. Jones, and if you are the Lytle Brothers, I'm hoping you can help me out."

"I'm Bud Lytle and this is my little brother Grover. What kind of help do you have in mind?"

"I need a car set up. Word is you two are the most successful moonshine runners in the state, so you likely have the best cars to do it. You would know who could set one up for me and keep it quiet."

Grover leaned forward. "And why would you need a car like that, C. O. Jones?"

"To conduct my business."

"And what business is that?"

Jones smiled. "Not the moonshine business, if that's what you're thinking. I don't want a tanker; I want a car that will, shall I say, keep me ahead of things. Call it a getaway car, if you like."

"And why would we want to help you in some possibly illegal enterprise?" said Bud.

"For the same reason most people do most things," said Jones. He lifted a hand from the table. "I'd like to get something out of my shirt pocket."

"Sure," said Grover, sliding a hand under the table where he likely had a sawed off shotgun mounted, pointing at the guest chair.

Jones reached into his shirt and pulled out a pair of hundred dollar bills. He held them up between his left thumb and forefinger. "I'm ready to pay for the information. Nobody rides for free."

Grover's hand came back to the table empty. He and Bud looked at each other and Bud turned to Jones. "And what would keep us from just taking that money from you and throwing you out the door?"

Like a magic trick, Jones flicked his right wrist and a .32 automatic popped into his hand on a spring from his shirt sleeve. "I'd say good common sense for a start." The brothers' eyes widened but neither moved. "Besides, you never know when a fellow like me might be able to return a favor. Can you help me?"

Bud looked to Grover and nodded. Grover hesitated a moment then nodded too. "You want Coakee," said Bud.

The pistol slid back up Jones's sleeve. "Coakee—is that a nickname?"

"Nope," said Grover. "Name's Earl Coakee. Has a place about two miles from here in an old barn. Bartender'll give you directions. We'll tell him you're coming tomorrow."

Jones laid the bills on the table. Bud shook his head and said, "Give that to Coakee if you and he get along, and he'll kick it to us."

"You can trust him to do that?" said Jones.

Grover smiled. "Sure we can. He's our cousin." He poured three drinks from the Mason jar. "Now that we're all friends, why don't you have a drink with us, C. O. Jones?"

The moonshine burned like lava all the way down, but Jones didn't flinch. Neither did the Lytle brothers. "By the way," said Jones, "you might want to find a better bouncer for this place."

"Can't do that," chuckled Bud. "Cecil's our cousin, too."

CHAPTER TWELVE

The next day Jones followed the directions the bartender scrawled on a matchbook. They led him to a good-sized barn on a back road that was all ruts and rocks for the first mile to discourage idle traffic then groomed like a ski trail for the second. The barn was as high as a two story house, sided with grey rough lumber. What might once have been cultivated fields around it now ran riot with ten years' growth of bramble bushes and sumac trees. When Jones pulled into the packed earth barnyard, three of the biggest, ugliest mongrel dogs he'd ever seen came running around the corner of the barn. The dogs barked and danced around the Pontiac, and Jones tapped the horn.

The man who stepped around the barn looked like a haystack in coveralls. He was tall, but his grossly fat body looked like a grey gumdrop on pillars. His face was almost as red as his hair, which hung in strings, melting seamlessly into his chest-long beard. He held a Colt .45 cowboy pistol at his side in his right hand and an open end wrench as long as his forearm in his left. The haystack gave a sharp whistle and the dogs shut up and sat beside Jones's door, eyeing him like an unattended steak.

Jones pushed open a wind wing. "Coakee?"

The big man nodded and stepped up to the car. "I guess you're Jones. You can get out. Dogs won't bother you long's you stay by me." Jones climbed slowly from the Buick, careful to make no sudden moves.

Coakee didn't waddle like many fat men; he moved with the kind of comfortable, heavy stride you might associate with a rhino or an elephant. He didn't gulp for air either. Earl Coakee was a man who had not only learned to cope with his size; he'd learned to do it without much effort. He pulled the sliding barn door to the side, and it rolled away more easily than Jones would have expected.

The barn's dilapidated appearance was a front for one of the most complete and pristine machine shops Jones had ever seen. The concrete floor was swept and spotless and the machinery gleamed. Tools hung from the walls in orderly ranks like the swords, spears, and shields of a medieval castle. Speedy would have been jealous. To the left, a half-dozen cars sat in various states of repair.

Two men, one in overalls and the other in work greens were elbow deep in the engine compartment of a '43 caddy. Neither looked up as Jones and Coakee entered, preoccupied with their work.

On an engine rack, Jones saw a flathead Ford V-8 like the one from his old '40 coupe, but this one sported two carburetors linked to the manifold by an odd-looking mechanism. "Centrifugal supercharger?"

Coakee nodded. "Sure enough."

"Where's this engine going?"

"Seems the dirt-track circuit is going big-time," Coakee said. They're organizing something called NASCAR, short for some long fancy name. They want to regulate racing and make it a national sport. I don't know how that might work out, but it can't hurt my business. Anyway, one of the local boys, Skunk Campbell wanted a go at it." Coakee crossed the garage to a car under a tarp. He pulled the cover away to reveal a '46 Ford two-door stripped to its body, frame, and wheels. The number 27 was painted on the side.

"So it goes in this one, eh?"

"That was the plan, but Skunk had a little run-in with the law last month, and he won't be paying any bills or driving any cars for about ten years."

"That's too bad. Did your cousins tell you why I'm here?"

Coakee nodded. "Said you needed a car set up." He pulled a pack of Luckies from his pocket and shook out one for himself and offered the pack to Jones.

Jones nodded his thanks and lit the cigarette. "I need speed and maneuverability, more or less what you'd build for a moon runner without the tank. But it has to look like a civilian machine."

Coakee's eyes shifted from side to side as he thought out loud. "That means less weight to haul, and less to fight around corners. The frame could be drilled out to lighten it some. Heavier torsion bars and shocks for less sway, beefed up springs, wider rims to put more rubber on the road to corner and stop better, and a hot engine. It could be done for the right money."

He pulled a set of keys from his pocket and threw them to Jones. He nodded to a maroon '38 Plymouth sedan. The car looked like something a family man might drive to church except for the pair of three-inch exhaust pipes under the rear bumper. "Let's see how you drive. Then I'll have a better idea what you need."

Jones slipped behind the steering wheel and Coakee heaved his bulk into the passenger seat. To Jones's surprise, the springs didn't sag an inch. He turned the key and almost instantly the motor rumbled into life. The clutch felt a little heavy as Jones let it out and the Plymouth rolled through the barn door and across the hard-packed yard.

"Go to the right out of the gate," said Coakee. "Short-cut to the highway." The sedan rode a little hard on the bumpy road, but the steering was firm. "We'll get on the blacktop in a quarter mile or so then you can cut her loose."

Jones stopped the sedan on the pavement. He held in the clutch and pushed down the accelerator, listening to the pitch of the engine. Jones eased out the clutch as he gave the car more gas and it leapt forward without burning rubber. He floored it and when he shifted into second, the transmission was perfectly smooth. Likewise third gear.

The Plymouth was doing about ninety when they hit the first turn. Jones drove through the curve across both lanes, making it two shallow turns instead of a single sharp one. He feathered the brakes as he spun the wheel against the drift. The car snapped in line as he hit the next short straightaway and floored it again. The next turn Jones allowed the car to drift in a controlled slide, never touching the brake pedal. He floored it again slingshotting out of the turn and soon the car topped a hundred.

Two miles later Coakee looked in a side mirror and said, "We got company."

A glance in Jones's rearview mirror showed him the flashing red light of a black and white police car. "Anybody you know?"

"Yeah, it's Lumpy Collins the local constable. He's a real crusader. No paying him off. His Chevy's got a pretty hot engine in it. You'll have to out drive him." Coakee's calm was unnerving; he was riding shotgun with an untested stranger at a hundred miles an hour and said "out drive him" as if he were lying in a hammock under a shady elm.

"He doesn't catch me he doesn't tag me, right?" Coakee nodded. Jones looked in the mirror again. "How close is the township line?"

"Not close enough. We won't be out of his jurisdiction for four or five miles of road the way it twists and winds."

Jones shrugged. "Okay, Coakee. Let's see how good he is. What's up ahead?"

"Two fairly sharp turns and a straightaway."

"Trees close?"

"Not particularly."

Jones rolled into the first turn and gunned the engine to accelerate out of the curve. Collins wasn't gaining on them, but he wasn't falling back, either.

The Plymouth rocketed out of the second curve at eighty-five. Jones held his speed steady. The constable slowed for the curve and stood on his gas pedal; the Chevy was gaining. He was counting on horsepower to make up for his lack of driving skill. "Hang on to your teeth."

Jones watched the road ahead with one eye and the rearview mirror with the other. He could hear the siren now over the roar of the Plymouth's engine as the Chevy gained on him. Ahead, Jones saw an intersection with a dirt road. His eye flicked from the pavement to the mirror to the speedometer. He had to time his move just right.

He wrestled the wheel hard left and the Plymouth went into a broadside slide. He double-clutched and wrenched the wheel again, throwing the car into second and barely making the right-angle turn onto the dirt road. Collins, startled by the move steered clumsily around the Plymouth, bounced onto the berm and shot past the intersection. He screeched to a halt and threw the prowl car into reverse.

Jones slewed the Plymouth left to right, churning dust as he went. At a wide spot in the road, he threw the car into a 180 spin, throwing up a dense cloud. As Collins drove into it, Jones drove out of it in the opposite direction, narrowly missing the prowl car. In a minute, the Plymouth was back on the blacktop putting space and time between itself and the Chevy.

Back at the barn Coakee said, "I didn't want to give you more car than you could handle. I guess I don't need to worry on that score."

"Want to just sell me this one?"

"Nah, this is my car. Besides, all the cops around here know it on sight. I'll fix you up one of your own. What make and model do you favor?"

"I've had my best luck with Fords, but you know the area and the roads. I trust your judgment." Jones pulled a roll of bills from his pocket. "A grand to start?"

Coakee nodded and slipped the money into a pocket of his coveralls. "I'll get on it today."

"And give this to Bud and Grover." Jones handed Coakee the pair of hundreds. "How's chances you build me an engine like that one?" Jones flicked his thumb at the supercharged V-8.

Coakee scratched his chin and his red beard waggled from side to side. "For what you want to do, that isn't exactly practical. Straightaways long enough to make that blower really useful are far and few between around here; lots of hills, lots of curves. You want to balance power with handling in a short space. Give me about two weeks. I'll fix you up what you need. You won't be disappointed."

Jones nodded and started for the barn door. Coakee said, "Better I go out with you. My dogs don't know the difference between customers and crooks. Some people are both."

CHAPTER THIRTEEN

That night after his workout, Jones came down the stairs to the poolroom and Bucky called him over. "Skitch wants to see you, Jones." He jerked his head to the back table where Skitch was running a rack by himself. "Grab a cue, Jones. Let's play a game or two."

Jones nodded. "I'm not the best at pool, but I guess I can hold my own."

Skitch grinned. "Spoken like a true hustler. Eight ball?"

Jones nodded and took a cue from the wall rack. He laid it on the table and rolled it from side to side. It was perfectly straight; no warping. The poolroom was dingy and the paint was peeling, but the equipment was all first-rate.

"Buck a game?" Skitch said.

"Sure."

"You break."

Jones broke and put in the thirteen and the five. He looked the table over. "I'll take low."

He ran the four, the one, and the seven before he missed a shot.

Skitch walked all the way around the table, eyeing the balls from every angle. He chalked his cue and rubbed a little excess off with his thumb. He reached into his pocket and peeled a dollar from his roll of bills. He wrapped the bill around the stick and worked it up and down, polishing the wood. He laid the bill on the rail and chuckled, "In case I lose." Jones saw a small red x beside the serial number. He pulled a dollar bill out of his wallet and threw it on top. "In case you win."

Skitch leaned over the table and drew back the stick. He stroked a gentle shot that threaded the cue ball through the low balls and past the eight to delicately nudge the purple-striped twelve-ball into a corner pocket. The cue rolled an inch or two and stopped in perfect position for a shot across the table to drop the ten. Next the fifteen fell an inch short of the side, and the cue ball nestled against the rail.

"Damn," said Skitch. "Just my luck."

Just mine too, thought Jones. The cue ball was perfectly located in the spot on the table least likely to give him a decent shot at anything. Jones tapped the cue ball and sent it off the far rail and into a cluster of balls, hitting one of his before the others.

Across the room, somebody made a better than average shot that drew cheers and jeers from the spectators. Skitch eyed the table and chuckled. "Got me in a spot, Jones." He walked around the table again, surveying the layout and bent over the side rail. "Don't know how this will work, but I'll give it a try." He low cued and the nine-ball rolled lazily into the other side pocket. The cue ball back spun out of the cluster and rolled to a clear spot on the table. The eleven went next and then the fourteen.

The eight ball was on the other side of two of the low balls, so Skitch played it safe and sent the cue through a tight two rail carom in the corner to gently kiss the eight ball and stop dead on the felt.

Jones had the two, the three, and the seven still on the table. He snapped the seven into a corner with a hard shot that stopped the cue ball dead on contact then dropped the two into a side pocket, leaving the eight ball between the cue and the three. Jones considered his options and sent the eight ball bouncing off the three. The three rolled for the corner pocket, but dragged on the rail and stopped an inch short.

Skitch shook his head. "Tough break, Jones. Good try, though. Other corner." With a smooth stroke, Skitch dropped the eight and won the game. He picked up Jones's dollar and left his on the rail. "Try again?"

Jones put down another dollar and broke. Nothing went in. Skitch walked around the table again, checking the angles, and Jones realized that it was all theater. Skitch could probably beat him blindfolded, but Jones played along, waiting to see where the scene was headed. Four games later, Skitch's dollar bill was still on the rail, and Jones was down five bucks. Every game was close but snatched away by Skitch just before Jones could beat him.

"Tell you what, Jones," said Skitch. "I'll give you a chance to win your money back; double or nothing and I'll shoot left-handed." Jones nodded. "Sounds like a good bet." He put a five on Skitch's dollar bill and the game began. Skitch broke again, and two low balls went in. "You know, Jones," said Skitch, lining up his next shot. "I like to shoot pool. It's a lesson in human nature. The game teaches me a lot about people; how they think, whether they plan, take chances, lose their cool—know what I mean?" He looked up.

Jones smiled. "What does it teach you about me?"

Skitch drove the four into a corner and the cue ball bounced off two rails to leave him a clean shot at the three. "That you're adaptable. You don't get flustered. You learn quick." He looked up. "And you're sharp. You've been studying me the whole time I've been studying you."

The three went in next, leaving the two, five, and six. "You show respect. You didn't ask me to put down a five to cover yours; you know I won't welsh on you for five bucks or five grand." A combination dropped the two and five. "What did you learn about me, Jones?"

"That you're as good at what you do as I am at what I do."

Skitch nodded. "I agree." He looked the table over. "Six in the side and eight in the corner." The cue ball nicked the six, which fell into the pocket, and spun at an impossible angle down the table through the maze of striped balls to knock in the eight.

"And it's not about the money," Jones said. "You really enjoy winning. That and you're left-handed."

Skitch laughed. "How about double or nothing and I shoot everything to one pocket?" Jones laughed too, and Skitch scooped up Jones's five and his original dollar. Skitch kissed the dollar bill and folded it into his vest pocket. "I've been betting the same dollar bill for twenty years." He put his cue in the rack. "A word of advice, Jones: don't shoot for money with my brother Dodie. He's better than I am. Come on with me."

Jones followed Skitch upstairs to the gym and past the guards to the elevator. Skitch stopped the car on the third floor. Jones looked out the door into a room lit by hanging lights like those over the pool tables downstairs. A poker game was going at one table with a mound of money in the center, ringed by seven men. At two more tables, men in shirtsleeves were dealing blackjack. A dice table, empty at the moment, stood away from the card games. There were more people at the tables than Jones had seen come through the poolroom or the gym, so he figured there must be somewhere else, maybe the basement, to get on the elevator.

"This is the game room," said Skitch. He waved to a man in a suit about a size too small for his shoulders. "Buckshot, come here. I want you to meet somebody." Buckshot was about six-five and Jones guessed his weight at two-seventy, little if any of it fat. His hair was buzzed close to his scalp and his eyes put Jones in mind of a Lynx. His hands were half again as wide as Jones's and the knuckles on both were scarred from plenty of front teeth.

Skitch said, "This is C. O. Jones. He's my guest." Buckshot nodded and Jones nodded back. He tumbled pretty quickly that the word "guest" was code for "he's allowed to be up here, but watch every move he makes." Skitch pointed to the ceiling. "We're going up to my office."

The big man stepped back and the elevator door closed. "We do the real business on the third and fourth floors," said Skitch. "The fire department's hook and ladder trucks can't reach past the second, so the cops can't use them to raid us." The fourth floor had men sorting piles of small paper slips on a group of long wooden tables. A desk with six telephones on it sat unoccupied, and behind it a racing tote board covered the wall. "This is where we write the numbers every day."

"A wire room too?" said Jones. "I'm impressed."

"We try to cover all the bases." Skitch led Jones across the room to a door at the far end. He opened the door and snapped on the light. The room was an elegant surprise. Unlike the bare wooden floors elsewhere in 220 Snowdon, Skitch's office was carpeted with a thick Oriental rug. The window that faced the Square was covered with good drapes, and the overhead light shone from a Tiffany shade. An oil painting of a city skyline that Jones recognized as Florence hung behind Skitch's desk. The work that went on in this office had little to do with pencils, papers, and adding machines.

Jones twitched. His tattoos were heating up like they always did when he was around magic. The score of runes and geometric symbols were there, as Hennessey put it, to "detect and protect, warnings and wards." He looked around the room but couldn't see anything obvious. Maybe it was in a desk drawer or a wall safe, but whatever it was radiated power like

"*This is where we write the numbers every day.*"

a beacon. Then he saw it: a statuette on a knickknack shelf on the far wall. It was about six inches high and made of what looked like tarnished silver; a horned man—maybe Pan, maybe Satan—something familiar.

The big desk shone like a new car. It was bare except for a telephone and a framed photograph of a woman and a small boy. Skitch saw Jones looking at the picture. "My wife Tillie and my son Frankie Junior. Sit down," said Skitch, gesturing to the chairs as he stepped around the desk. "What time is it?"

Jones looked around the room but couldn't find a clock.

Skitch smiled. "I noticed you didn't wear a wristwatch. I wondered whether you carried a pocket watch instead like most of the railroad guys."

Jones shook his head. "I haven't worn one for a while. There's usually a clock handy."

Skitch opened a drawer in the desk and took out a cigar box. "A man needs a good watch these days to stay on top of things." He set the box in front of Jones and opened the lid. It was filled with wristwatches. Some had leather bands in various stages of wear, a few the newer expansion bands in gold and silver. Some of the brands Jones recognized from Europe, like Speidel and Gruen and others from America like Hamilton and Bulova. Jones raised an eyebrow.

"They aren't hot," said Skitch. "The guys who put them up for cash in card games weren't hot either. And if you ever decide to get married..." Skitch set a smaller box on the desk. It was full of gold and silver rings, most of them plain gold bands.

"Looks like there are a lot of sad stories in that box, Skitch," said Jones.

Skitch nodded. "Yeah, but it's just business. Anyway, you need a watch. Pick one out for yourself."

Jones hesitated. "I'm superstitious about obligating myself. How about I buy one from you? Say for a dollar?"

Skitch's brow furrowed. "A dollar?"

Jones held up Skitch's dollar bill with the red X by the serial number. Skitch dug into his vest pocket and laughed out loud. Jones smiled. "Close quarters in the elevator."

"I'll be a son of a bitch. Jones, you're full of surprises."

"It's kept me alive up to now." He handed Skitch the bill and rummaged through the cigar box. He picked out a heavy Gruen pilot's watch on a thick leather strap. The face had 3, 6, 9, and 12 in Arabic numerals and the 13-24 military hours on a tight circle inside and seconds in fives on the outside. "How about this one?"

Skitch grinned. "You got me fair and square, Jones. Sold."

As Jones buckled the Gruen onto his wrist, Skitch said. "So, how did a person with your expertise end up working the coal dock in Brownsville, Pennsylvania?"

"Brownsville was recommended to me by a former employer."

"And what sort of work did you do for this employer?"

"I was a cleanup man." Jones's expression went flat. "You know the term."

Skitch nodded. "You contract to handle messy situations for the big boys. Things they need resolved but can't touch themselves. Kind of a troubleshooter."

"That's one way to describe it."

"How did you get into that line of work?"

"You know the story; the Army trained me to break things and kill people, and once the war was over, I came back and found there was only one business that needed my odd set of skills."

"But you don't hire on permanently."

Jones shook his head. "I'm not a family man. I like my freedom."

Skitch nodded. "I respect that. And I'll respect your privacy. But you came to us, so does that mean you're available if we need you?"

Jones nodded. "Yes. And if I sign on, I won't sell out to a higher bidder, say somebody like Mickey Malone."

"And if somebody wants to hire you against us?"

"You've been square with me, Skitch. And this is your town. Let's say I'll give you first option if I can."

"Fair enough."

"Before we go back downstairs, Jones, just one more question: were you really in the Army Air Corps?"

Jones laughed. "For about two weeks, then I was, let's say, reassigned."

CHAPTER FOURTEEN

Reassigned: a simple word for making a simple life complicated.

Twenty minutes after his interview with Colonel Hennessey, the newly minted lieutenant was carrying his duffel bag to the Jeep. The barracks was empty. Based on what he could see of the equipment, the company was out on a full-gear forced march. Nobody to say goodbye; they wouldn't miss him. He couldn't tell any of them where he was going anyway. He didn't know it himself. Simmons stood alone at the doorway and looked down the silent ranks of two-deck bunks. A month ago he'd walked away from the life he knew and today he was walking away again; a new day, a new life, a new man. No looking back.

The M.P. drove him across the base to the airfield and a waiting plane. It was a two-prop Douglas Skytrooper, a model Simmons recognized from his early instruction in the Air Corps. The Skytrooper was a stripped down version of the Douglas DC-3 passenger airliner; all the utility and none of the comfort. Simmons sat alone in the passenger compartment. All this plane for one soldier? Its twenty-eight seats were metal plates welded to the frame parallel to the sides of the hull, and the lack of interior paneling and carpet made the cold metal tube resonate with the throb of the engines. An hour in the air gave Simmons a splitting headache. Two more hours didn't make it go away, either.

It was night when the Skytrooper touched down. The plane had made so many turns and corrections that Simmons had long since lost any sense of direction. A sergeant in a flight suit opened the side door and told him he had ten minutes for the latrine and a smoke while the plane refueled. When he stepped out of the outhouse at the end of the runway, he looked around him. There was a dark nothing as far as he could see. Just like his future. If he ran for it, he didn't know if there was a fence a hundred yards away or half a mile, or nowhere. And now that they knew what he was and he knew at least a little of what they were about, no matter where he ran, they wouldn't stop until they found him again. Just ride it out, he thought. What else can I do?

The sergeant handed him a brown paper sack and a thermos flask. "Here are some sandwiches and coffee. Sorry we don't have time for a regular meal, Lieutenant." Lieutenant. It would take a while for Jones to get used to that.

Four hours in the air and the plane touched down again. Another M.P. with another Jeep was waiting and drove him along darkened streets. They cruised through a tall brick archway, and as they did, Jones could read the words scrolling overhead in wrought iron: Duke University. The Jeep crossed the shadowed campus and stopped in front of a two-story brick building dwarfed by the Gothic spires of the buildings around it.

"Follow me and bring your gear." The M.P. led Jones through double doors to a desk manned by a corporal. The M.P. handed him a file folder that looked like the same one Hennessey had leafed through earlier. "Here's the new boy."

The corporal nodded and picked up a phone. He did more listening than talking, and the call was over in less than a minute. He stood and saluted. "Welcome to Duke University, Lieutenant Simmons."

After sleeping in the barracks with his company, the quarters were luxurious: single occupancy, private bathroom, and air conditioning. The other side of the coin: barred windows and no handle on the inside of the door. The Army wanted him to stay put, and he didn't seem to have a choice. He set his duffel at the foot of the bed, stripped down and stood in the shower for a half hour. Five minutes later, he was asleep.

In the morning after breakfast (which was brought to his room by a staff sergeant with a sidearm), the new lieutenant was taken downstairs to a set of rooms in the building's west wing. For three hours a trio of white-coated doctors gave him the most thorough physical he'd ever experienced. They drew blood, took urine samples, thumped his knees, measured his skull. The doctors looked at every inch of his body. Then after lunch in his room he was taken into a windowless laboratory full of scientific gear he couldn't name, and cameras and microphones. A different gang of white coats ran him through a battery of tests, some written, some oral, some performance.

The doctors made Simmons do his card trick over and over, timing him with some kind of fancy chronometer. They had him try to call the cards from the other side of a wooden partition, then steel, then glass. If he could see the action, he could see its outcome. Behind mortar, wood, or metal, the Sight didn't work. They tried other tests on him. Could he see colors blindfolded, in the dark? Behind him? Could he read thoughts? Could he move objects with his mind? All negative. They took his watch and shut him in a featureless room then asked him at various intervals what time it was. They interviewed him three times that afternoon, asking him the same questions in ten different ways. By the end of the day he was exhausted physically and mentally, and his head felt as if it were in three pieces.

Dinner was a steak and baked potato with corn and green beans on the side. They even threw in a beer. The tests were a bitch, but he couldn't complain about the rest of his situation. For the next three days, the people in the lab coats poked and prodded his body and his mind. Simmons found it tedious, but he had to tolerate it all. No options.

The fourth night the desk jockey from downstairs took him to an office where Colonel Hennesey was waiting, the open green folder on the desk in front of him. His file was twice as thick now, likely padded with the test results. Simmons saluted and Hennesey returned it offhandedly. "Sit down, Lieutenant."

Hennessey looked back to the folder and read for a moment then closed it and folded his hands on it. "Has everyone been treating you well?"

Simmons nodded. "Yes, sir. The food's great and the room is comfortable."

"I meant the testing and examination."

Simmons nodded. "Not bad, but I really don't understand it all."

"You will soon, Lieutenant, because you have been deemed suitable for the special unit. You ship out for training tomorrow morning. Ever hear of Camp X?"

Simmons shook his head and Hennessey went on. "Most people haven't because it's a closely guarded secret. It was set up in Canada by the Brits to train operatives for their military intelligence before we ever entered the war. Once we signed on, they saw the value of sharing resources with us, and we started sending men up there to prep them for special missions. You'll be taught a hundred ways to kill with weapons and a hundred ways to kill with your bare hands. You'll be taught how to operate every piece of equipment available to the military—on both sides—and some that only a handful of us have ever seen. When you're through, you'll be ready for the most important job in this war, and in this century, for that matter."

"The Nazis are trying to corner the market on what? Witchcraft? Magic? I don't understand why this is so important."

"Ever go to church, Lieutenant? Read the Bible?"

"Yeah; I read it when I was a kid in Sunday school."

"Ever hear of Auschwitz?"

"The German death camp? Yeah, I've heard about it."

Hennessey's stared across the desk and his voice took on an intense timbre: "All those Jews the Nazis are gassing at Auschwitz? That isn't genocide. Hitler's sacrificing Jews to Moloch for victory."

CHAPTER FIFTEEN

A few days later a call came for Jones at Snowdon Square. He was upstairs working the heavy bag when Bucky came up from the poolroom. "Jones," he yelled over the clank of the weights and the thumping of the bags. "Telephone downstairs."

Jones wiped his face on the sleeve of his jersey and followed Bucky down the steps. The old wall phone was behind the counter, the earpiece sitting on top of the box. "This is Jones."

"This is Coakee. Car's ready."

"That was quick. I'll have to catch a ride up there. Tomorrow okay?"

"I'll be here all day."

"What's the freight?"

"You come up and try the car then we'll talk money. Who knows? You might not like it." He chuckled.

"I doubt that," said Jones. "See you sometime tomorrow."

"Tell you what, Jones, meet me at Bud and Grover's bar. The less people know where my shop is the better."

"It'll probably be after work. That a problem?"

"Not for me. See you then."

Jones hung up the phone and went looking for Danny Hayes.

The next afternoon, Danny dropped Jones off at the backwoods beer joint. At the end of the lot next to Bud and Grover's Merc was a navy blue '42 Ford Coupe. As he got out of the car, Danny said, "You need me to wait for you?"

Jones shook his head. "No need. I expect I'll be driving back."

Coakee, in his coveralls, sat at a table with Bud and Grover and an Iron City Beer when Jones walked in. Coakee waved him over and shouted over the jukebox, "Car's outside. Did you see it?"

Jones said, "Blue '42 Ford Super Deluxe?" He laughed. "I thought it belonged to some shoe salesman."

Coakee and the Lytles laughed with him. "That's the whole idea," said Coakee. "But looks are deceiving. Let's take her out." He turned to Bud and Grover. "You want to ride along?"

Bud shook his head. "Too crowded in the back. That's a car for two people."

Grover added, "Or two and a half if Coakee's riding shotgun."

Coakee waved the joke aside with a grin and said to Jones, "Let's go."

The coupe stood a few inches lower than standard height. "I did channel the body a little to give it a lower center of gravity, but it looks stock at first glance. I figure it'll fool the average copper. It'll corner fast without rolling. This model doesn't have running boards, but I figured you didn't want extra riders tagging along anyway."

Coakee walked around to the front and reached under the hood for the latch. "I think you'll like the engine." He raised the hood and Jones whistled in appreciation.

The entire engine compartment was perfectly clean. The flathead block was painted bright red and the headers were gleaming silver. "Finned the headers," said Coakee. "They cool better. The engine's stroked a quarter and bored an extra eighth of an inch. I put in domed pistons for more compression, and I put heavy springs on the rocker arms. She'll idle a little bit rough when she's cold, but at two thousand RPMs she'll purr like a sewing machine. Never hurts to let the oil heat up before you really push her, but I figure you know that. Two carbs and a hot ignition coil. The intake manifold's ported. I figure it pushes the horsepower from the original ninety to about a hundred fifteen."

Coakee closed the hood and walked around the back of the coupe. Below the bumper twin exhaust pipes showed. "Twin pipes with mufflers for driving around town, and alongside the steering wheel there's a cut out switch for straight pipes under the rocker panels. I put in steel rods to protect the radiator and the bumpers are reinforced with I-bar through to the frame. There's a slider plate, half-inch steel to protect the gas tank. It all added a few pounds, but if you get rammed..."

"I get the idea. Good thinking."

"Trunk latch opens from under the dash. Handle's a dummy, and the trunk is reinforced like a strongbox. You'd need a stick of dynamite or a torch to pop it open."

Jones rounded the side and opened the driver door. The interior looked stock except for a slightly longer gear shift lever rising from the transmission hump.

"Keeps your hand closer to the wheel. And here..." Coakee reached in and flipped up the dashboard heater grille revealing a group of toggle switches. "You have shut off switches for the individual head and tail lights; keeps the cops guessing. Run with one headlight off then while the cops are looking for a car with one light, you drive home with both of them on. And this switch is an ignition override. You can start it without the key from here and if you turn it this way, nobody can start it even with the key."

Coakee tripped the catch and pushed back the driver's seat. He peeled back the carpet and Jones saw the edges of a lid with a pull ring. Coakee flipped it up to reveal a twelve-by-twelve inch compartment three inches deep. "I put it near the driver's seat so you can get to it while you're driving if you have to."

Jones shook his head in admiration. "Coakee, you're an artist." Jones pulled out his roll of cash. What do I owe you?"

"Don't you want to test her out?"

"I think that would be an insult to your genius."

"You gave me a thousand up front," Coakee said, scratching his chin. "Give me another six hundred and we'll call it square."

Jones nodded, peeling bills from the roll. "Sounds fair to me. And when I need a tune-up?"

Coakee pulled a parts receipt from his pocket and scribbled a number on it with the stub of a pencil. "Any time you need it, call this number. They'll get word to me. And Jones..."

"Yeah?"

"You take good care of her. These cars are like children to me, and I'd hate to see one of them come to a bad end." He handed Jones two sets of keys on a chromed ring. "If you need another set of keys, come see me. The local Ford dealer doesn't have this pattern in stock. Keeps out the unwanted."

Jones took the keys with his left hand and offered his right to Coakee. Coakee's grip was like a hydraulic press, and Jones decided that he'd never want that hand around his throat. "Thanks, Coakee. Pleasure to do business with you."

Jones started the engine. He listened for a moment to the deep growl, put the car in gear and pulled out of the lot onto the rutted dirt road. Now, he thought, the crate.

CHAPTER SIXTEEN

At Brownsville's Union Station, Jones handed his claim check to the clerk and in five minutes, he came out of the warehouse with the crate on a dolly. "Had to look for it, mister," the clerk said. "It's been back there a few weeks and got covered up with other stuff."

Jones tipped him a dollar and lifted the crate to his shoulder. In two minutes, it was in the trunk of the Ford and Jones was headed out of town into the country. He drove around the back roads for a half hour until he found what he wanted. The old farm was a quarter mile off the road at the end of an overgrown lane. The house was caving into itself and the barn was missing half its roof and siding.

He pulled behind the barn in case someone drove by and took the crate into the ramshackle building. He pried the lid away with a tire iron and pulled out the green canvas sack. Inside it, pipes clattered together. The largest ones were three feet long and four inches in diameter, the ends closed with threaded caps. He read the markings and lifted out one of the pipes. He unscrewed its cap and reached inside to pull out a pair of sawed-off .12 gauge shotguns packed in machine oil.

Jones chose the double barrel and slid the three-shot pump back into the pipe. He fitted the scalloped aluminum pistol grip behind the trigger housing, making the weapon look like an oversized musket. He cleaned the shotgun thoroughly with shop rags he'd lifted from the roundhouse, and after he finished, he set it aside and chose another pipe.

Inside it, Jones found a dismantled Sten gun packed in oil like the others. He cleaned and assembled the Sten then loaded a pair of clips; thirty-two rounds of 9 millimeter ammo each. Jones fitted the suppressor over the barrel and took the Sten outside. He pulled back the cocking handle and fired a few quick bursts at a dead tree nearby. The gun spat and the tree trunk splintered as the slugs tore through it. Some Stens jammed at inopportune moments, but this one was fine tuned by MI5's top armorer.

Stens were a lighter and more easily concealed alternative to the Tommy guns American gangsters preferred—and try carrying an extra magazine for a Thompson .45 in your back pocket. Sure, they didn't hold as many rounds as the Tommy gun, but shooting men was more often a matter of quality rather than quantity.

Other four-inch pipes held a dozen fragmentation grenades, two M-1s, a Mauser sniper rifle, and more than a thousand rounds of different calibers of ammunition. A smaller pipe was filled with gold coins from a dozen countries. Another held a collection of bayonets and knives of every type.

Jones cleaned the Sten's bore, reloaded the clip, and put it along with the shotgun, ammo, and three of the grenades in a compartment behind the Ford's spare tire. He put the pipes back into the waterproof bag and buried it in a corner of the barn under a rusting disc harrow. He sat back, lit a cigarette and read *A Farewell to Arms* until the sun set then drove back to Snowdon Square, ready to go to work when the time came. Skitch knew what he was, and Jones figured it wouldn't be too long before he'd need his services.

CHAPTER SEVENTEEN

In the poolroom, a group of men clustered around Skitch and a small boy, the one Jones had seen in the picture upstairs; dark haired and dark eyed, he was the image of his father. "Hey, Jones," Skitch called, "Come over here a minute. I want you to meet my son." Jones sauntered over and the boy suddenly stopped laughing and looked up at him with wide dark eyes. Jones felt his tattoos itch. Something about the kid. "Frankie, this is Mister Jones."

"Hi, Frankie."

"We're celebrating. Frankie picked a winner for us." He beamed with pride. "We took him upstairs, and Richie told him to pick a number from one to ten, then a second, then a third: 726. We played it for a laugh, and guess what—it hit." The boy still stared at Jones, unsure what he was feeling.

"Hey, kid, c'mere." Jackie the Leg beckoned to Frankie. The spell broken, Frankie ran to the familiar face away from the strange one. Jackie was perched in one of the tall chairs against the wall. He pulled up his pant leg and opened the side of his artificial limb. He pulled out a roll of bills and peeled off two ones. "Here's a dollar for picking a winner," he said, "and here's a dollar for being a good kid." Frankie took one in each hand, and turned, proudly showing off his booty to his father.

"That's my boy," said Skitch crouching and holding out his arms. Frankie ran into them, and Skitch scooped him up and hoisted him onto his shoulder.

"Hey, Skitch," said Dodie, "bring him back tomorrow and we'll clean up."

"Tillie'd strangle me in my sleep," he laughed. "She reads me the riot act every time I bring him here as it is. I'll have to drive around with the windows down for an hour before I take him home to blow the smoke off him." Everybody had a laugh at that, and Jones started for the stairs to the gym. "Hey, Jones," Skitch called to him. "You gonna be here a while?" Jones nodded. "I'm taking the boy home, and coming back. Stick around, will you?"

Jones nodded. "I'll be here." He was right. Work was on the way.

Upstairs, Tommy Cimino was in the ring sparring with Eddie Lewicki, a kid who was short on technique but long on enthusiasm. He was charging Tommy with salvos of punches, hoping one of them would land in the right spot. Jones decided that for the locals sparring with Cimino was like calling out the fast gun in the Old West. When you're King of the Hill, everybody wants to push you off even if he's only on top for a glorious minute before somebody else knocks him down.

Fats, his jowls waggling, was bellowing at Tommy in his gravelly snarl. "Step wide, keep him turning, damn it! You want him to tag your jaw?"

Lewicki landed a lucky one below Cimino's eye and sent him staggering backward. It broke the skin, and blood welled out of the cut. Fats nodded to one of the ring rats. The bell gonged, but Tommy didn't quit. Jones saw a sudden flash of anger in his eyes and fear in Lewicki's. Tommy threw combination after combination at the kid's head, cocking his headgear askew. Lewicki put his gloves in front of his face and Tommy hammered his torso. The bell rang insistently. Fats was screaming now, and Lewicki was backing into a corner. "Get in there! Pull them apart! Tommy! God damn it!"

Tommy was screaming now too, as he pounded Lewicki mercilessly. Lewicki turned into the corner and Tommy was punching his kidneys. He was still swinging as two of the men dragged him back and Fats heaved his bulk under the ropes. Fats ripped of Tommy's headgear and shouted into his face, "Hey! Hey!" Fats slapped Tommy hard, forehand and backhand blows that swiveled Tommy's head on his neck. "Settle down, damn it."

Tommy's chest heaved. His breath came in ragged gasps. Fats snarled, "What the hell you think you're doing here?" He put a thick finger in Cimino's face. "You can't control yourself now, how do you think you're gonna handle Rodgers? Damn it, Tommy."

Tommy sagged, his head down, like a chastised child. "I—I," he stammered.

"Shut up!" then in a controlled voice that was more menacing than his bellow, "Get out of my face." Fats turned his back, his jaws clenched. "Go back in the locker room and get Max to dress that cut."

The men let go of Tommy's arms, and he tumbled, shell shocked, out of the ring. In the corner, Lewicki was curled up on the canvas against the post. The men set him upright as gently as they could and helped him under the ropes. Jones heard one of them say, "Sit him down in a chair out here. Don't take him in the back 'til Tommy's gone."

Jones had seen it happen many times before in combat. Too much adrenaline; shock, pain, and anger brewed a hard mix to swallow. Nothing more dangerous than losing control, he thought. If Cimino couldn't handle it, his future would likely consist of breaking legs for Skitch until somebody put a bullet in his head. Jones looked across the room and saw Tommy's wife, her hands clenched white knuckled over her unborn child, and in her eyes, a look of unbridled horror at a side of her man she'd never seen before.

Jones worked with the dumbbells that night; low weight and high reps. Keep the tone but add no bulk; don't get muscle bound and lose agility. After an hour of concentrated work, he showered, dressed, and went downstairs to shoot pool and wait for Skitch.

He played a few games with one of the loafers downstairs, won fifty cents and lost a quarter before Skitch came in. He motioned for Jones to follow him and started up the stairs to the second floor. By the time Jones caught up with him, he was waiting by the elevator. He skipped the third floor and rode to the top. The room was busy when the stepped out of the cage, men working at the long tables, some punching numbers into adding machines, others counting out payoffs. A lot of people played 726 that day.

"How about that, huh?" said Skitch. "Frankie guessing the winner."

"He ever do that before?"

"Naah, we just do it for laughs. Every time he comes down here we have him pick three numbers. Probably never happen again."

Don't be too sure, thought Jones, thinking that the statuette in Skitch's office somehow amplified some latent ability in Frankie. He'd seen it happen before. "Was he up here when he picked the number?"

"Yep, sitting right on my desk, why?"

Jones shrugged. "Maybe it's a lucky spot, but you know what they say about lightning."

"Ain't that the truth," said Skitch, unlocking his office door.

In the office, Jones felt the power radiate even stronger from the grey statue than before. Maybe it drew power from Frankie, and maybe it was drawing power from him.

"You have a really motley crew here, Skitch. Jackie lose that leg in the war?"

"Naah, he was in the pen when it started. He lost the leg in a car crash before he went in."

"And he always carries your money?"

"Yeah, and everybody knows it, but they all know better than to try to take it. At least they do now. One night two young punks got ambitious and tried to jump Jackie when he got out of the car at his house. They came out of the bushes and sapped Sal and knocked Jackie on the ground. They were trying to pull off his leg when he slashed one of them across the throat and shivved the other one. Story is they took a midnight swim in the Mon."

Jones shrugged. "I guess you don't survive the joint on one leg by the force of your personality."

Skitch offered Jones a cigarette and they both lit up. "So, Jones, you interested in a little easy money?"

Jones smiled around the cigarette. "Who isn't?"

"One of my men. Little Johnny Santello's running a big card game in Republic tomorrow night and my driver Jerry's got a personal beef with

Little Johnny." He snorted. "Woman trouble. I need somebody to trade off with Sal upstairs at the game and down at the door while Dodie and I play. Job pays a hundred if we win big, twenty if we don't. Do you have a suit?"

"No, but I can get one easy enough," said Jones. Skitch reached for his bankroll and Jones put up his hand. "No need for that. I can afford it."

Skitch nodded. "Okay. Go to Carlo Giaconda's tailor shop on Water Street. I'll call him and tell him to expect you. He'll take care of you right away. Be here tomorrow night at eight o'clock."

Jones was almost out the door when he turned and offhandedly said, "By the way, I was curious about that statue. I saw one like it once—a bigger version when I was in Europe during the war."

Skitch lifted the statue from the shelf and held it out to Jones. "Guy came in here two months ago and had a bad run at the poker table. He put it up for four hundred bucks and lost every dime."

"Stolen?" Jones took the statue in his hands and his tattoos got warmer. It wasn't silver, platinum or pewter. It was way too heavy for its mass. It radiated force to Jones like a beacon. The slanted eyes in the horned head seemed to bore into him.

"Who knows? I don't ask." Skitch put the statue back on the shelf. "You say you saw one like it in Europe?"

"Yeah," said Jones, but it was marble and it was a lot bigger."

CHAPTER EIGHTEEN

In fact it was taller than two men and standing behind an altar in an underground temple near Munich. Jones's alias was Gerhard Reinhold (code name Wormwood), and his OSS partner (code name Dutch boy) was Jan Hutz, under the name Alex Gestettner. The two were disguised as German bureaucrats on holiday, supplied with the best forged papers and plenty of Marks to spend.

Under Hennessey's direct order for security reasons, no one in the unit spoke much about his special talent or asked others about theirs, so Simmons wasn't certain why the agent was paired with him at first. But he soon deduced that speaking any language Hutz heard was his gift; not just parroting, but like the apostles of old speaking in tongues. It was as Dutch Boy could reach into a person's head and pluck out his vocabulary, syntax, and inflection.

"It radiated force…like a beacon."

Hutz was a drinker, a gambler, and a ladies' man whose blonde hair, blue eyes, and boyish features made him irresistible to a certain breed of woman. Simmons was no prude or teetotaler, but on assignment, he tried to stay focused and avoid distraction.

"Hey, we're on holiday, right?" said Hutz. "We have to play the role. I say eat, drink, and be merry." And he did.

The intelligence that led the pair to the torch lit cavern cost plenty of money and a few lives, but it was accurate. Hutz and Simmons, wearing SS officer uniforms, evaded the perimeter guards and boldly approached the three sentries at the cave's entrance. Recognizing higher rank, they snapped to attention. "Where is Oberst Grauben?" Hutz said to them sharply in flawless colloquial German.

"Sir, there is no Oberst Grauben here."

"Is that so? We were told we would find him in this hell hole. He is a traitor, a spy. Are you perhaps hiding him? Delaying us while he makes his escape?"

The guards looked at each other in anxious confusion. Hutz sneered. "Look at me when I speak to you, not at each other. Now tell me, where is Oberst Grauben?" The guards stared at Hutz as Simmons stepped quietly behind them and thrust needles tipped with cyanide into the necks of the two within reach. Hutz plunged a knife into the throat of the leader, slashing his windpipe before he could cry out.

Simmons and Hutz dragged the bodies out of sight and stealthily entered the cave. It was a natural cavern, water-formed limestone with stalactites pointing from its ceiling. The formations gave the impression of walking into a mouth full of jagged fangs. The floor was sand, and had been dug away to make the descending passage taller. Flickering torches hung from the walls at irregular intervals leaving stretches of light and darkness.

A hundred feet in, the passage turned sharply to the left, and Simmons and Hutz drew their pistols, standard issue Lugers. They could hear faint chanting and dissonant music up ahead, that and footsteps approaching. Each pressed to a different side of the passage in the darkness and waited. In a moment, two men in red robes, hoods pulled back from their heads, rounded the corner. Simmons leapt from the shadows and clubbed one with the butt of his pistol, and he fell to the floor unconscious. A twist of his head snapped his neck. At the same time Hutz whipped a garrote over the second man's head and pulled it tight. In a moment the man was dead.

Five minutes later, Simmons and Hutz, wearing the red hooded robes of their victims, followed the sound of chanting. The further they went, the harder their tattoos throbbed, and the hotter they became until Simmons was afraid they would burn through the robes and give them away.

The cave opened into a high domed grotto whose ceiling was lost in shadow. In its center loomed the pagan statue leering down at a stone altar. On it were three dismembered bodies, at least one a child, limbs and torsos arranged in some odd runic pattern. In the center of the grisly emblem a priest in a robe with the hood back and a golden diadem on his head stood behind a man seated in a chair, back to the statue. The priest raised his hand for silence and the chanting ceased. He held a large knife aloft, murmured an incantation, and made a series of ritual cuts on the seated man's torso, the red blood welling darkly against his pale skin.

The seated man began to tremble, slightly at first, then violently, then not at all and he began to speak in what Simmons recognized as Greek. The voice was much deeper and louder than a human's, and Simmons marveled that it didn't tear out the man's vocal chords or burst his chest. The words echoed powerfully throughout the cave, but Simmons heard them inside his head and understood them with perfect clarity as if they were spoken in English. "Who summons me?"

The priest knelt and put his head to the stone of the altar. "Your obedient servant, who humbly offers you the gift of threefold sacrifice and begs you share your wisdom."

"What question do you bring to me?"

Hutz hissed almost inaudibly, "It's a God damned oracle."

The priest rose and turned to the idol. "How may the Reich succeed in waging this war? What must we do to ensure victory?"

The voice boomed, "You must not permit a feinted blow to draw your strength from the true attack. I see danger. I see a great army coming from land and sea and air. *Uberlord!*"

Hutz drew his pistol and put a bullet through the medium's throat, silencing him. Simmons fired a shot though the back of the priest's head, sending the diadem spinning in a glittering arc. Before the hooded worshippers could respond, one grenade landed at the base of the statue and another at the entrance to the grotto. Bullets whizzed by the Americans and Jones felt the sting as one grazed his ear.

The explosions were deafening in the cavern, but Hutz and Simmons threw more grenades in the hope of caving the passage in around their pursuers. Stalactites, shaken loose by the concussions, fell like spears impaling some of the robed Nazis and pinning them to the sandy floor.

The Sight tingled, and Simmons saw one of the calcite spears pierce Hutz as he turned to fire at the enemy. Simmons threw himself at Hutz in a cross-body block and pushed him aside, rolling when he hit the cave floor to barely escape the calcite spear. One last grenade proved to be too much for the stone and the walls of the cave collapsed near the entrance, trapping the pursuers in the tunnel.

The cave swallowed much of the sound of grenades and gunfire, but enough got out to attract the attention of the outlying sentries who rushed to the entrance. The scarlet robes confused them long enough for Simmons and Hutz to run out shouting, "Inside quickly! Intruders!" The guards rushed into the cave mouth only to be cut down by machine gun fire from the fallen sentries' weapons.

Simmons threw off his robe and leapt onto a motorcycle parked nearby. By the time he'd kicked it into life, Hutz was on the back, and the pair roared off through the trees into the darkness as more grey-clad soldiers ran into the clearing, too late to catch them, and too late to save the underground temple.

"That was too close to the truth to be an act," said Hutz later at their debriefing. "That idol, or demon, or whatever it was had Overlord pegged. We took that one out just in time." Both of them had been sketchily briefed on the massive invasion plan and were sent, as were other teams, to prevent supernatural interference. Theirs was but one of a number of similar missions with similar results.

Hutz chuckled and looked across the table at Hennessey. "And someday when my kids ask me, 'What did you do in the war, Daddy,' what do I tell them?"

Hennessey, unsmiling, leveled his gaze at Hutz and said, stonily, "You tell them you won."

CHAPTER NINETEEN

When Jones got up the next morning, he pulled the newspaper under the door and into the room. Marty was reliable. He hadn't missed a day since Jones put him on the payroll. He turned the paper over and saw the headline: Berlin Airlift Begins. Predictable, thought Jones. It's Russia's turn to be aggressive and the U.S. can't help but play the role of good guys. But at least the Russkies don't have the atom bomb. Just a matter of time, I suppose. He tied his shoes and headed to Fiddle's for breakfast.

At the roundhouse he stopped by the office to see Hankins. The boss hadn't ridden him too hard lately. Maybe he was doing a good job. Maybe word got around about his fight with Tony Motsko. Maybe Hankins heard he was working for Skitch on the side. Maybe Hankins saw the butt of his automatic under his shirt.

"I need to leave an hour early today, boss, maybe two." Jones could have gone to the tailor on his lunch hour, but he didn't want the coal dust and dog sweat fouling his new suit.

Hankins sat forward in his chair. He opened his mouth to speak, then didn't for a long count. He thought it over and said, "No earlier than four o'clock, right?" Jones nodded. "Don't expect me to pay you."

Hankins is braver than he looks, Jones thought with a chuckle. "Didn't expect you would, boss," he said and without another word turned and headed for the dock. Jones shoveled straight through lunch and at four o'clock he headed for the gym to shower before he went to Giaconda's shop.

The tailor shop was nestled between a florist and a grocer. Inside, Jones found a small man with a fringe of white hair reading a newspaper behind the counter. "Mr. Giaconda?"

The little man put down the newspaper and Jones saw a small pistol beside him on the counter. "Jones?"

Jones nodded, and the little man jerked with his thumb to the back of the shop.

Jones stepped through a curtain and found a middle aged man pumping the treadle of a sewing machine. A round belly pushed through his unbuttoned vest. Carlo Giaconda puffed on a dark crooked cigar in an ivory holder as he worked, white brows furrowing with concentration. Jones waited for the man to speak.

"Skitch says you need a suit quick." His accent wasn't as heavy as some of the immigrants he'd met in Brownsville, but it was obvious that Carlo Giaconda wasn't home grown. He spoke around the cigar over the chattering of the Singer without turning his head.

"Yes, sir, I do."

Giaconda nodded and the machine stopped. He stood and stepped back from Jones, looking him over and sizing him with his thumb the way a painter would gauge proportion. He walked around Jones, put both hands on the caps of his shoulders and patted his chest. "I got you." He disappeared around a corner and came back with three used suits on hangers. "Try this." He handed him a Navy-blue chalk-striped mohair with wide lapels.

Jones stepped into the dressing room. The suit wasn't bad but it was a little tight across the shoulders. Carlo tugged here and there, walked around Jones and shook his head. "Maybe this one." The second suit was a dark grey pinstripe in a light wool that fit as if it were made for him. "You like?"

The little man from the front counter came back and said something in Italian and he and Carlo laughed. Carlo turned to Jones. "He says the suit looks good on a live one. Most of the used ones I sell to the funeral parlor. Like all the suits I do for Skitch, low arm holes, room to carry."

Jones looked at himself in the full length mirror. From the neck down he looked like a bank president. "Yeah. This is good. Feels right." Carlo looked at his feet. "You not wear those shoes." He pointed to Jones's work-scarred brogans. He spoke in Italian again and in a moment the little man returned with five shoeboxes under his arms. "Skitch says you need a suit. I say you need the whole outfit."

Jones found a pair of glossy black oxfords that fit him while Carlo chased down a white shirt and a wine red necktie with white stripes. A black fedora finished the ensemble. "What do I owe you?"

"You work for Skitch; the whole thing: thirty dollars." Jones gave him forty over his protests. Carlo had to make a living too.

CHAPTER TWENTY

Jones pulled up to the poolroom in the Ford at 7:30; better to be early than late, he thought.

Danny came out and whistled as Jones stepped onto the sidewalk. "Good looking car, Jonesey." A lot of the guys in the gym and the poolroom had picked up on the nickname, but Jones didn't mind. It made him fit in better. Danny walked around the Ford admiring it. "I liked the wedge grille in the '39 better than the flat one in the '41, but she looks good. What's under the hood?"

"V-8," said Jones without giving details. "Runs real smooth."

"Nice." Danny nodded, took another drag on his cigarette and followed Jones inside.

At that moment Skitch and Dodie came down the stairs with Sal who dragged a short man by the collar of his shabby tweed sport coat. "You don't understand!" the short man cried. "I have to have it back!"

"Then come up with the four hundred and you can have it with my blessing, Mike." Skitch shook his head in disgust. "Throw him out," he said to Sal, who hauled him to the doorway and pitched him onto the sidewalk. Mike picked himself up and through the window, Jones saw a look not of anger on Mike's face, but of desperation.

Skitch spotted Jones and waved him over. "Time to go," said Jones to Danny.

As they walked out of the poolroom, Jones said to Skitch, "If you don't mind me asking, what was that all about?"

"People don't understand the concept of hocking their goods. That's Mike Donovan. He's the guy who gave me that statue you saw in my office for credit. He kept losing and I kept the statue. Now he wants it back. Like I said once before, it's just business."

Skitch looked Jones up and down. "Carlo fixed you up good," he said. Then quietly, "You carrying?" Jones nodded. "Never had trouble at Little Johnny's game before, but there's always a first time."

They rode to Republic in Skitch's Buick. Jones sat in front while Sal drove. The whole eight miles Dodie and Skitch argued over which team would win the National League pennant. The discussion was no idle chatter. The Yankees were almost a sure thing for the American League, but the National League was up for grabs and betting would be heavy. They still hadn't settled the dispute when Sal pulled into a parking space in front of a three story brick building. The ground floor was taken up by Vitelli's Plumbing Supply, and what appeared to be apartments occupied the upper floors. Everyone got out and walked to the side of the building.

Sal rapped on the door and it opened a few inches. An eye peered out, a chain latch rattled, and the door swung inward. Arnold the doorman was a big dumb lout with a crooked nose and a cauliflower ear. Jones decided that the mob was the last stop for old pugs. Made sense; they weren't afraid to take a pounding and they never forgot how to throw a punch.

Skitch walked in first. "Arnold," he said, "how's your brother? Is he out of the hospital yet?"

Arnold smiled sadly. "No, Mister Mottola, and the docs think he might not make it."

Skitch patted Arnold's thick shoulder. "I'm sorry to hear that. I truly am. If there's any way I can help you or the family, you tell me, you hear?"

Arnold nodded just a little too fast. "Yes, sir. Thank you, thank you, Mister Mottolla."

"You know Sal." Arnold nodded again. "This is Jones. He'll be down here on the street for a while and then he'll be coming upstairs later." Then to Jones, "Stand outside the door, and if you see anything looks wrong; cops, whatever," Skitch pointed to a doorbell button two feet into the doorway. "That's the alarm, in case Arnold hasn't buzzed it already."

"Anything else I need to know?"

Skitch shook his head. "This is a well-run game. I just like to know we have somebody watching our backs."

Skitch, Dodie, and Sal started up the stairs and Jones stepped back into the alley. "That Mister Mottolla, he's a nice man. He always asks about my brother Ralph," Arnold said, before closing the door. Skitch should have been a politician, thought Jones. Then he decided that there was really little difference.

Jones took a position at the corner of the building where he could see the alley and the reflection of the street in the display windows of a dress shop on the other side. The night was quiet. A few cars rolled past, dogs barked, and for a few minutes, some harridan lit into her husband for being a lazy drunk. Otherwise, two hours passed with little to break the monotony. Sal stepped out the side door and called Jones over.

"I'll take the street for a while. Skitch says for you to go up. There's food and drinks. Just keep an eye on the game."

Jones climbed two sets of dimly lit stairs and found himself on a landing facing a steel door. He rapped on it with his knuckles. An eye slit opened and a pair of eyes peered out. "Yeah?"

"Jones. I'm here with the Mottollas."

The eye slit closed. In a moment, he heard a thick metal deadbolt slide back and had to step back as the door opened almost the span of the landing. Can't break that one in without dynamite, thought Jones. A hood in green pants with red suspenders over a black shirt and a .38 in a shoulder rig motioned him in.

As soon as he stepped into the room, Jones's tattoos started to itch.

The room was big and in its center a round table stood under a shaded hanging light. Skitch sat the table with six other men. All were in shirtsleeves, cuffs rolled up; insurance against extra aces. The dealer was a young kid with wavy hair and wire rimmed glasses. Jones watched as his spidery fingers shuffled and cut then walked the three of clubs across the back of his hand, finger to finger. He showed the card around the table. "Blocking card, three of clubs." He turned the card face up and put it on the bottom of the deck.

"That's Joey, Ice," said Dodie over Jones's shoulder. "He can deal you an ace off the top, off the bottom or out of the middle, and even if you watched him do it, you'd never know. He can read a marked deck like you and I read a newspaper. Johnny keeps him on the payroll because he's reliable and because nobody cheats better than he can."

"He's that good, huh?"

"Maybe even better; if he spots a cheat, Joey deals him a Joker. The cheat has one chance to fold and walk away or the next hand Joey deals him eights and aces."

"Dead man's hand, huh? Then what?"

"Little Johnny's boys take him outside."

"Which one's Little Johnny?"

"He's not at the table. He just hosts the game. That's him in the corner."

A short, squat man in a shabby black suit stood away from the table. His thick glasses made his eyes owlish. Every minute or so he mopped his forehead with a handkerchief like a nervous habit. Jones found it hard to imagine Jerry competing with Little Johnny for the same woman, but sometimes power and money trumped good looks.

The room opened through twin screen doors onto a porch. A hundred feet up the hill in the parking lot behind the Riviera Hotel Jones saw a two men standing behind a parked car. One of them had binoculars trained on the doorway. "Looks like you have spectators."

Dodie laughed. "They're here every week. By the time the cops get past Arnold, up the stairs and through that steel door, the cards and cash disappear and we're playing Monopoly. The cops know this is a high stakes game, but they still have to make a show. Sometimes I think they leave the game alone because it keeps us all in one place so they know where we are."

"You aren't playing?"

"I was, but I dropped out. Skitch and I are both losing big tonight. Skitch is down maybe two grand. Armenian Sam's cleaning up. His luck comes and goes, but the last couple of weeks he's been winning more. Tonight he can't do wrong. Raises when he should, folds when he should, never misses a bet."

The Armenian looked more like a toad to Jones than anything else. His skin was a pale shade of yellow, maybe the tag end of jaundice. Watery brown eyes peered from under heavy lids. His thick jowls drooped into his shirt collar, and he breathed through his slack mouth. Armenian Sam didn't have much hair on his head, but the hair in his ears and nose could make a decent wig for somebody.

Jones poured himself a whiskey, passing on the ice. He'd acquired a taste for Old Overholt rye during the war when it was the unofficial medicinal alcohol of the U.S. Navy, and Jones was surprised to learn that it was distilled in nearby Connellsville. He carried his drink over and watched the game for a while. Skitch bet big on queens and aces, but the Armenian raised him and won the hand with a full house. The next hand, Skitch had three jacks, and the Armenian folded before the pot got too big. From behind Jones could see he had three nines.

Joey Ice looked across the table to Little Johnny. Johnny raised his eyebrows in question and Joey answered with a shrug. If something was up, neither could see it. But something was up, and Jones could feel it. He moved closer to the Armenian and felt the tattoos pulse just a little stronger. There was no big magic working here, but there was magic.

Dodie said quietly, "I've been watching him. There's no shiners, and I can't see any way he's marking the cards. If he was denting the aces, Joey would feel it in a second."

Jones stepped back and watched as Joey Ice sent the red and white bicycles on the card backs spinning end over end, five to a player. Everyone anted up and while they looked at their cards, the Armenian rubbed his forefinger and thumb around a silver ring on his pinky. The player to Skitch's left opened but the bets were small. After the draw, the Armenian fingered the ring again, and Jones was certain that was his gaff. Armenian Sam bumped up the pot and won the hand with a full house.

When the next hand was dealt, Jones took a step closer to the Armenian and another, not obvious, just random kibitzing, and he saw Sam's brow wrinkle in confusion. The nearness of Jones's tattoos interfered with the ring's magic just like jamming radar. Sam desperately rubbed the ring like Aladdin's lamp, but no genie appeared to show him the other players' hands. Jones saw panic on his face. The Armenian lost that hand and the next three. Sweat trickled down his jowls and into his collar. He wanted to get up and leave more than anything in the world, to run away from the game he was now losing, but if he did, the other players would suspect what Jones already knew. Cheats rarely lived to spend their winnings.

Jones sipped his whiskey and watched the Armenian slowly collapse into himself like a deflating balloon. Can't blow the whistle, thought Jones, because then I'd have to explain how I knew. Better to let the game run its course without any more rigging.

By the end of the night Skitch won back his money and more besides. So did everybody else. The only big loser was Armenian Sam. He'd won a few hands, but nothing to recoup the pile of money he lost. Jones would have felt sorry for him but pity had deserted his emotional repertoire long ago. Putting on his suit jacket, Skitch said, "I'll have to bring you along next time, Jonesey, you're good luck."

Jones smiled. "No such thing, Skitch. We all make our own."

As they rode back to Brownsville, Jones tuned out the conversation, preoccupied with who had magic and what he should do about it. The Armenian was just a user, probably a cash cow for somebody else's benefit. He didn't know what he had, only that it worked. People out there in the dark were shuffling the big cards, and if Jones smelled them, it was a good bet that they smelled him.

CHAPTER TWENTY-ONE

Two days later, Jones pulled the paper under the door and turned it over to read the headline: "Local Businessman Murdered." The photo accompanying the article showed a younger Armenian Sam holding a police booking card across his chest.

The article was brief and blunt. The corpse of Sero "Sam" Artinian was found on the east bank of the Monongahela River near his Brownsville printing shop Tuesday, dead of multiple gunshot wounds. Despite Artinian's criminal record and reputed ties to the underworld, Police Chief Edward Bronson says that simple robbery was the likeliest motive. "His watch and wallet were missing. It's pretty obvious." He stopped short of "good riddance."

It could have been little Johnny's boys, taking out the cheat, but it was more likely something a little darker. I'm betting they took his ring, too, thought Jones. Poor sap.

It was an easy scene to imagine. Bad people get their hooks into you. Maybe you run up a lot of vig on a loan. Maybe they get the goods on you for something you've done. Or maybe they just find your weakness. They play you like a fish and once you take the bait, they own you forever. They offer you a sure thing, give you a slice, and when it goes south, you become an embarrassing loose end and they have to cut off the finger before it points back at them.

But whoever gave the Armenian the loaded ring was still out there, and close. Too close. Part of Jones told him to take off, find another town, maybe a big city where there was more room and less likely collision. Another, stronger part of him told Jones that no matter where he went, there would always be more of it; better to stay and deal with it for good or ill. Step around it if you can, or fight it if you can't.

Magic was just another version of the mob, thought Jones; force, intimidation, power, and it lurked as an undercurrent in every town and village everywhere. The war against the Japs and the Nazis was done, but the war Hennessey pulled him into would never end, even when the last man fell.

"It's always been here, like a hybrid branch of physics," Hennessey once said, "since before there were humans. It's like gravity or electricity or the wind. They're neither good nor evil. You can't see any of them, but you see what they do. And they'll still be here when we're long gone. And like we use electricity or gravity or the wind, we can use magic. The difference is that to use magic, we need a channel, an intermediary, somebody or something who's been in the game forever, call them gods, demons, whatever you like, and those somethings play for keeps. That's where evil enters the picture."

Jones was convinced that the Sight was not magic; it was just something in his brain that pointed sideways instead of up and down. But what Hennessey introduced to him and the others in the Unit was something else altogether. Like the Armenian, he'd been hooked, maybe shanghaied was more like it. But Hennessey and the OSS taught the Unit just a little too much, trained them just a little too well, and allowed them to see a little bit more than they should have.

When the war ended, Hennessey tried to keep the Unit together. Or maybe Uncle Sam just wanted to maintain such valuable resources all in one kennel for future reference. Like the atom bomb we were a threat to the world, thought Jones, but we were their personal assignable threat. In balance, we were too dangerous to allow us to live, but like the bomb, what we could unleash at our destruction was more dangerous still.

In the throes of war, the OSS was short-sighted. The supernatural booby traps they wired into the Unit's operatives against enemies worked as efficiently against them. The demon that used pieces of Hennessey to decorate the walls, floor, and ceiling of his office sent a message to that effect. The Unit scattered and Jones hadn't seen any of them since and really didn't want to. The Army, after a few horrific incidents, learned to leave them all alone.

But the Nazis had magic, and the Brits had magic, and the Japs had magic. Everybody had magic. You could push it down here or there, but like gravity, electricity, or the wind, it never really went away. It was always lurking over the next hill and always would be.

Jones threw the newspaper on the unmade bed. Time to go to work.

By the day's end, Jones had made up his mind. There was no point in running. When magic shows up, you deal with it. You join it, you fight it, but you can't run from it because it will chase you like a hungry wolf no matter where you go once you've shown weakness. It wants to eat your power. The magic was small, this time, and if he was going to survive, Jones had to find its source and confront it before it grew.

He was almost at the hotel when a voice called to him. "Mister Jones?"

Jones turned to see a small barefoot black boy, wearing patched overalls with no shirt over his bare chest. "Yeah, kid, I'm Jones." The boy looked around him to see who else might be within earshot then looked Jones square in the face. Jones was startled to see that one of his eyes was brown and the other green. Satisfied no one else could hear, the boy grinned and said, "Granny Maybelle says to tell you the bad thing be here, and worse be coming."

His message delivered, the boy turned and ran down the alley. "Hey, kid, come back," Jones called after him. "Who's…?" He cut off his question realizing that people across the street were staring at him. He looked down the alley and saw no trace of the boy.

As he climbed the stairs to his room, the questions buzzed around his brain like hornets. Who was Granny Maybelle? How did she know him? What bad thing was the kid talking about? Was this connected to Armenian Sam?

The answer to the last question was obvious. When magic is involved, everything is connected.

CHAPTER TWENTY-TWO

That night at the gym, Jones pulled Danny aside and asked him, "Who is Granny Maybelle?"

Danny started to laugh then realized Jones's question was a serious one. "Granny Maybelle's an old colored woman lives outside town across Redstone Creek. She's a healer for her people and some of the poor whites who can't afford a doctor. Some of the folks around say she's a witch. Why do you want to know about her?"

"I heard somebody mention her name at the diner. Just wondered who she was."

"She's the lady to see if you want your warts cured, or gout or the shakes. And she'll brew you up a love potion if you need one, or send you a dream to find something you lost."

"You ever go to her?"

Danny looked away for a second then back at Jones. "Once, a couple years ago. My girl friend Sadie threw me over for another guy. I was really broken up about it, and somebody suggested I go see Granny Maybelle. I was lovesick and figured what the hell. She made up a potion for me—cost me five bucks—and damned if Sadie didn't come back. But when she did, she clung to me like a drowning man to a life preserver. It got so I couldn't go out for a pack of smokes without her hanging on me."

"Overkill, huh?"

Danny laughed. "It got so I couldn't stand the sight of her, and I went back to Granny Maybelle and said, "Please call it off.""

"And did she?"

He chuckled. "Yeah, for another ten bucks. I guess the lesson is to be careful what you wish for, huh? Maybe it was all hooey, but maybe it wasn't, because the next day Sadie threw a skillet at my head and she was long gone."

"So Granny Maybelle's the real McCoy?"

"Plenty of folks think so, and some of the worst people in Brownsville step out of her way when she walks down the street. I guess it's better to be safe than sorry, huh?"

Jones nodded. "That's always a good policy, Danny."

He pounded the speed bag for a half an hour until sweat dripped from his brow. As he worked out, Jones thought hard about everything he saw and heard the past few days. And Brownsville seemed like such a simple place. Something worse is coming, he thought, and I didn't even have to prick my thumbs.

CHAPTER TWENTY-THREE

Two nights later, Tommy Cimino was set to fight Jack Rodgers in Madison Square Garden for a chance at Sugar Ray Robinson's welterweight boxing title. Robinson had been undefeated for five years and had held the title since 1946. He'd logged over eighty knockouts since turning pro, and although it was a long shot that a contender would beat him, a shot was still a shot and worth fighting for.

The poolroom was empty that night; everyone was upstairs in the gym gathered around a big Philco radio tuned to the fight. A washtub bristled with beer bottles in ice, and every fist in the place was holding one. The

Cimino-Rodgers fight was third billing, one of the preliminary bouts for Tony Zale's third try at Rocky Graziano, but to the Snowdon Square crowd and the people of Brownsville, Tommy's fight was the most important bout in the world that night.

Sportscaster Eddie Martin's voice boomed over the radio. "And tonight, two Pennsylvania boys go at it for a shot at the welterweight title. The winner of this bout is guaranteed a matchup with Sugar Ray Robinson." The fight was three hundred fifty miles from the gym, but for the electricity in the air, you'd have thought it was in Snowdon Square's ring. The ring announcer's high-pitched nasal voice echoed through the radio as if he were in the room.

He read off the pedigree of the referee, the attending physician, the judges and the time keeper then said, "In this corner, wearing red trunks weighing 146 pounds, from Geneva, Pennsylvania, Jack Rodgers and in this corner wearing white trunks, weighing in at 143 pounds, from Brownsville, Pennsylvania..." The gang in the gym yelled and whistled before Tommy Cimino's name was even mentioned, and Jones realized how much devotion the men held not just for their champion but for their hometown.

Martin said, "Tonight the middleweight title fight is the main draw, but some real drama is taking place right now between these two young boys, evenly matched and both itching for a chance at Sugar Ray for the welterweight title. Two young men, Rodgers twenty-seven and Cimino twenty-four, bodies like Greek statues, and grim determination etched on both their faces as each realizes his whole life has narrowed to this place and this moment. And now referee Marty Beck is giving the fighters their instructions."

"Gentlemen, you received your instructions this afternoon in the office of the New York Athletic Commission I remind you, keep your blows up; no low blows, no kidneys, no rabbit punches. And when I tell you to break out of a clinch, I mean just that. I want you to break clean and step back before you start punching again. And remember, gentlemen, any infraction of these rules may cost you the round, or even the fight. I want you to protect yourselves at all times. Shake hands now and I want you to go back to your corners and come out fighting at the bell." It was a litany they had all heard many times before but necessary. Now it was official.

Martin said, "And now, we'll hand the microphone over to Don Dunphy to call the fight. Dunphy's voice was higher pitched than Martin's but had an edge of insistency to it that made you listen. "The rivals have shaken hands and are now in their corners waiting for the bell. A reminder to the listening audience: this fight is sanctioned by the New York State Athletic Commission and will be scored by the standard ten points per round by the judges. The stools and seconds are out of the corners now, and the fighters are stretching at the ropes, getting ready for what promises to be an exciting bout.

"And there's the bell." The crowd at Snowdon Square roared encouragement to Tommy as if he could hear them all the way in New York. "They're dancing in at each other," said Dunphy in rapid fire, "and Cimino's wasting no time, delivering a wicked combination to Rodgers' chin, but Rodgers pulls back just in time to avoid major impact. Rodgers' feet are as quick as his fists, and he circles and tags Cimino with quick jabs at his nose."

Dunphy's colorful language and bullseye descriptions painted a vivid moving picture for the audience. "Cimino backs away and now it's Rodgers' turn to attack. He's stepping forward, leading with his left, jabbing at Cimino's face with every step, and Cimino is backing away, gloves up, trying to circle away from the ropes. The punches are landing hard, folks, and they sound like a ball bat on a side of beef.

"Cimino throws a hard jab at Rodgers' face, but Rodgers twists aside and the punch connects with his left ear. He'll grow some cauliflower from that one. They're circling now, more cautious, dancing out of each other's reach. Rodgers has a few inches on Cimino, but it doesn't seem to count for much against the ferocity of the Brownsville boy's attack. Cimino steps in to throw a left under Rodgers' elbows and Rodgers pops Cimino with a short jab just over his eye. Rodgers tries for another, and Cimino ducks his head. Rodgers' punch slides over Cimino's scalp. And there's the bell ending round one in this hotly contested bout between two Pennsylvania welterweights, Jack Rodgers and Tommy Cimino."

While Eddie Martin touted the virtues of Gillette blue blades and safety razors, Jones got another beer from the tub. He pried the cap away with a twist of his thumb and forefinger. Danny's eyebrows raised in surprise. Jones shrugged. "It's all in knowing how."

"That's a good trick," said Danny. "You'll have to teach me how to do that sometime."

The judges scored the first round for Rodgers, and at the start of round two, the pace of the fight picked up. So did Dunphy's running account. "There's the bell, and Rodgers bounds out of his corner, determined to show Cimino who's boss. Rodgers throws his right, two, three times, each

"Cimino throws a hard jab..."

one catching Cimino on the shoulder. Cimino bobs and comes up with a left that grazes Rodgers' jaw. Another jab to the nose and Rodgers is stepping back. Cimino dances in, weaving, keeping his hands moving, looking for his shot.

"Rodgers hooks with his left at Cimino's forehead as Cimino bobs his head out of reach. Cimino stepping in now, jabbing at Rodgers' ribs, keeping his left up. Oh! A right hook from Cimino catches Rodgers' left cheek. Rodgers comes back with a combination left right, the left catching air but the right gets Cimino just over his left eye. Cimino's cut; blood is running down his face. He bobs back and Rodgers follows him, pressing his advantage. Left, right, left right from Rodgers and holy mackerel! Rodgers tries for another combo and Cimino slips the third and catches Rodgers in the jaw with that right hook. Rodgers reels. Cimino steps in with a combo of his own and Rodgers hits the canvas!"

The gang in the gym roared, and Jones thought, the kid's got control of himself. He might win this one yet.

Somebody turned up the radio so everyone could hear Dunphy's voice over the shouting. "And the count: three, four, five, six, and Rodgers is up in seven. The crowd's going crazy. Marty Beck holding up fingers in front of Rodgers. Cimino's dancing in his corner, just itching to go at him again. Beck steps back and the fighters move in and there's the bell, end of round two. And these men go their corners knowing that at this moment it could be anybody's fight."

At the gym, more beers and more backslapping. Jones hadn't seen such enthusiasm since VJ Day. "What do you think, Jones?" said Danny. "Think he'll win it?"

"Like the man says, could be anybody's fight, but the kid's doing good."

Commercials over, Dunphy resumed his coverage. "The judges have awarded the second round to Tommy Cimino. It's a great match, ladies and gentlemen; two fighters in their prime, both with one eye on each other and the other eye on the prize, not the money but a title shot at Sugar Ray Robinson. No matter what happens later tonight, it'll be hard to overshadow the contest we're seeing here and now. And there's the bell.

"Rodgers comes out of his corner, a little less aggressive this time, a little more wary of Cimino now, and Cimino moves in leading with his left high. Rodgers plants a hard one on Cimino's chin! Cimino steps back, his gloves dropping and Rodgers moves in. Cimino twists to the right and shoots through Rodgers' gloves – a solid hit over his left eye. Rodgers is bleeding! He staggers back, and Cimino's on him every step, pounding his midsection and driving him into the ropes."

The crowd at the Garden was as enthusiastic as the gang at the gym, but Jones was sure he could pick out Fats's bellowing voice, and maybe Skitch's and Dodie's too amid the roar. But the voice Jones didn't hear was Roseanne, Tommy's pretty young wife. Was she sitting ringside gnawing her knuckles, or was she waiting with the unknown back in the locker room counting beads on her rosary?

"Rodgers rolls out of the ropes and dances just out of Cimino's reach as Cimino tries that vicious right hook again. Rodgers retreating as Cimino wades in jabbing, watching for his chance. They're circling now, like two tigers in a pit. Rodgers is buying time to catch his wind, but Cimino's on him every second, watching for a clean shot.

"Rodgers throws a hard right to Cimino's ribs and," Dunphy paused for a second, either to catch a breath, or from sheer surprise. "And Cimino shoots his left over Rodgers' right and lands a hard shot to Rodgers' chin!" The crowd at Snowdon Square screamed, sloshing beer on each other as they waved their fists in the air. "Right to the head! Right to the head! Cimino's punishing Rodgers!

"Rodgers comes off the ropes, and he and Cimino are in a clinch. Referee Marty Beck is pulling them apart. Cimino dances to his corner, and Rodgers, obviously shaken goes to his with less steam. Thirty seconds left in round three. Cimino charges Rodgers and – wait! Cimino is suddenly looking around, bewildered, swinging wild at nothing! Rodgers is standing back, hesitant. His corner man is screaming for him to move in and he does, but slowly, cautiously as Cimino turns in a circle throwing punches at the air almost as if he were shadowboxing. Cimino's shouting something! He's shouting, 'I can't see!' Folks, Tommy Cimino is blind!

"There's the bell. The third round is over, but there may not be a fourth. Cimino's corner man Dave Brigatti and his trainer Fats Mungo are in the ring now, leading Cimino to his stool. And there's the ring doctor on his way to Cimino's corner. He's holding up his hand in front of Cimino's face. He's talking to Fats Mungo."

The crowd at the Garden roared like a waterfall, but at Snowdon Square the cheering had ceased like someone slammed a door. The stunned silence in the gym was broken by a lone voice that summed up the feelings of everyone in the place: "Holy shit."

"And the doctor's examining Tommy Cimino again. None of the hits Cimino took looked to me to be bad enough to do that kind of damage, but every human body is unique. Rodgers is waiting in his corner for the doctor's determination. The doctor is waving his arms criss-cross in front of his chest. Fats Mungo is throwing a towel into the ring! They're calling off the fight! It's over!

"Jack Rodgers gets the title shot in one of the strangest fights I've ever seen! Tommy Cimino, going great guns but apparently blinded in the bout is out of the running, maybe forever. Beck is holding Rodgers' hand up in victory, and Cimino's corner men have him by the elbows, helping him out of the ring."

Danny snapped off the radio. "I think we heard enough." The gym crowd began to silently drift toward the stairs. The party was over.

"Damn," said Danny to Jones.

"Fortunes of war, Danny," said Jones, but in the back of his head, Jones was adding two and two and getting five. There was another piece to this action. Jones couldn't see it yet, but he was going to find it.

CHAPTER TWENTY-THREE

Brownsville was in shock. The *Telegraph* ran the headline "Blinded Cimino Forefeits Bout." Everybody heard it. Everybody read about it. Nobody discussed it.

Skitch and Dodie came back the next day, leaving Tommy Cimino in New York with Roseanne and Fats. The hospital wanted to keep him for observation because the doctors couldn't determine exactly why his eyes quit. There was no physical damage that they could find, and the word some of them were using was "psychosomatic." One smarmy headshrinker argued that maybe deep down inside Tommy was afraid of winning because he feared failure against Sugar Ray. Fats didn't fear failure when he knocked out three of the shrink's teeth.

Jones didn't see Skitch or Dodie around the poolroom for a day or two. They were apparently licking their wounds and paying off some heavy wagers on Rodgers. Jones found Skitch shooting alone when he came down from the gym. He walked back to the corner table and leaned against the wall while Skitch finished running the table. "Hell of a thing about Tommy," said Skitch. Jones nodded. "I know he wanted it," Skitch said, "I mean, he wouldn't throw that fight."

"The docs found no dirty tricks? Nobody put something in Tommy's water bottle? Rodgers didn't rub something in his eyes off his glove?"

Skitch shook his head as he dropped the balls into the triangle. "Nope, and the kid's still as blind as a mole. Grab a cue. Let's shoot a couple."

Jones took a cue from the rack and said while Skitch chalked his stick, "If we can't figure out how, maybe we can figure out who. The first question I'd ask is: who won big on the fight?"

Skitch looked up and said, "A lot of people. Rodgers bragged that he'd take the kid out in three rounds, and a dozen or so guys bet anywhere from a hundred to five hundred that Rodgers would do it. The odds were steep. We couldn't lay off much of it, and we took a big hit."

"Any chance they were proxy bets? Say for Malone maybe, trying to break you?"

"Dodie and I thought about that. Maybe that's the way it went, but we can't prove it."

"Give me a couple of names of the winners. I'll look into it." Jones broke and the balls scattered all over the table. Nothing went in.

Skitch walked around the table sizing up his best shot. "I can do that. Does this mean you're on the payroll?"

Jones shrugged. "We can talk about that later if you like, but for now, let's keep it unofficial."

Skitch put in the three and the seven with a neat caroming shot. "I'll have some names for you tomorrow."

CHAPTER TWENTY-FOUR

The next two days were quiet around the pool hall and the gym. Everyone was down in the mouth because of Tommy Cimino's loss. Jones went to work at the coal dock as usual, and another shovel man came and went. The second night instead of going to the gym, Jones started looking for the first man on Skitch's list of lucky bettors, Frank Hyatt. He made a stop at the Western Union office where he took a couple of blank telegram forms from the customer desk and headed on his errand.

Hyatt lived in a cold water walkup on Broad Street, about three blocks from Jones's hotel. He wasn't home at six o'clock, so Jones settled down on a bench across the street to read an ASE paperback of *Treasure Island* and wait. In an hour or so, a guy in a cheap suit strolled down the sidewalk and stepped into the doorway to the stairwell. Jones watched the second story windows and in a moment, a hand raised the sash on one of them.

He slipped the book into his pocket and walked a block to the next corner where he crossed the street out of sight from the apartment windows then walked down the sidewalk close to the buildings. The stairwell door was unlocked and through the glass Jones saw one mailbox: Hyatt. He took the stairs quietly and stood in the hallway for a moment, listening. From inside he could hear a bad radio playing a scratchy rendition of Glenn Miller's "String of Pearls." He rapped on Hyatt's door.

Jones heard a shuffling noise from inside, footsteps approaching the door, and the sharp click of a switchblade. A voice said, "Who's there?"

"Western Union—telegram for Frank Hyatt."

Jones heard the key turn in the lock. The door opened a crack – the chain latch was still in place. Jones held the telegram forms, barely visible in the dim light of the hallway, at eye level. The door opened a little wider, and Jones kicked it in. The door caught Hyatt in the face and he went over backwards, dropping the knife on the floor. He tried to get up but by the time he had rolled over, Jones planted a knee in his back. He grabbed Hyatt's necktie from behind and yanked it around to the back of his head. Jones held the knot in one hand and pulled at the short end with the other.

Hyatt struggled. Jones tightened the silk noose. Hyatt got wise and stopped struggling. Jones held the tie tight with his left hand and grabbed a handful of Hyatt's oily hair with his right. He pulled Hyatt's head back far enough for them to look each other in the eyes. The music on the radio changed to Guy Lombardo's version of "I'm Confessin'." Jones smiled grimly at the irony. "You don't know me, Frank Hyatt, but I think we have an acquaintance in common—Mickey Malone?"

Hyatt's eyes widened. He made a gurgling noise in his throat. Jones said quietly. I'm going to ask you two questions, and you're going to answer me. I'll know if you're lying, so don't even try it." He yanked on the necktie for emphasis. Question number one: Did you lay down a bet on the Cimino-Rodgers fight for Mickey Malone?"

Hyatt gurgled again and Jones said, "Just nod or shake your head." Hyatt hesitated for a second then shook his head side to side. Jones yanked on the necktie. "I don't believe that's true. Let's try again. Did you bet on the Cimino-Rodgers fight for Mickey Malone?" This time Hyatt nodded jerkily. Jones loosened the knot and Hyatt gasped for air like a fish in a rowboat.

"Question number two: what was your cut of the action?"

"Ten—ten points," Hyatt stammered, his voice ragged.

Jones looked down at Hyatt. "You're really stupid, you know that? I bet if you asked for twenty, you'd have gotten it." He yanked the necktie tight again. "Listen close, Frank Hyatt. I never came here. You never talked to me. Got it?" Hyatt nodded again, his eyes wild. "Remember, I caught you alone this time. I can do it again." Jones let go of his hair and drove his fist behind the right hinge of Hyatt's jaw. The thug went limp, and Jones loosened the necktie.

He left Hyatt where he fell and closed the apartment door behind him. On the sidewalk he pulled Skitch's list out of his pocket, read the next name and address, and headed for his car. The next guy, Sam Mercante, lived across town along the river on Water Street. Jones parked a block away and stood outside the clapboard house. The porch sagged, and a corner of the screen drooped out of the storm door. A tricycle sat on the sidewalk near the front steps. It was twilight now, and lights were on in different rooms of the house. Jones stood at the end of the walk and thought it over. Hyatt hadn't seen him; in this neighborhood there were plenty of people around who'd tell the cops all about him if he got rough. As he turned to leave, an old Mercury pulled up in front of the house.

The man who got out was short and heavy, dressed in a sport shirt and grey slacks whose knees shone like polished granite. He was carrying a sack of groceries in each arm and he pushed the car door shut with his rump. As he walked around the car from the driver's side, Jones stepped up behind him and put the barrel of his pistol behind his ear. "Sam Mercante, don't turn around." Mercante froze. "I'm not going to hurt you or your family if you just tell me one thing: what percentage of the take did Mickey Malone give you for placing his bet on the Cimino-Rodgers fight?"

Mercante stood perfectly still, a sudden trickle of sweat running from his cap to his nose. "Ten."

"You never spoke to me, and I never heard you say that," said Jones. "Now go in your house, Sam Mercante, and enjoy dinner with your family."

Mercante took a long breath, and without turning around, walked across the sagging porch through the torn screen door. But if he had disobeyed, it didn't matter. Jones was nowhere to be seen.

It was the same story from two more of the bettors on Skitch's list. So Malone tried his way to hurt Cimino through Motsko and to hurt Skitch and maybe take over his operation. When that gambit failed, Malone found another way: magic. There was no way Malone was the source, thought Jones, otherwise, I would have felt it the first time I saw him. It's time to dig a little deeper.

Jones parked the coupe on the street near the hotel and instead of going up to his room he started walking; one block north, one west, one south, then two east. Then he changed his pattern: one north, one west, one north, one east, one south, circling block after block in a zig zag pattern.

He walked for two hours until he'd covered a good chunk of the north side of Brownsville above the river. No dice. He didn't feel even a tingle from his tattoos. Wherever the magic was working in Brownsville, it wasn't in this neighborhood.

Back in his room, Jones lay on the bed and stared at the ceiling. In the war magic was about power. But in Brownsville, it seemed to be about money, maybe as a means to power. Asking who in this town wants more money is like asking who breathes, Jones thought. Someone supplied Artinian with enough push to win at cards. Did the same person bankroll Mickey Malone's wagers then rig the fight so Cimino would lose? Jones wanted to know, not out of some sense of right and wrong, or even some sense of loyalty to his employer. Someone had thrown a snake into Jones's bed. He'd found a place to live and work, to get away from magic. Now, someone was sneaking it into small town life like pouring poison into the village well, dragging him back to everything he left when the war ended.

Jones sat up in the bed and turned out the light. "Find it and fight it," he said, and rolled over and went to sleep.

CHAPTER TWENTY-FIVE

The next night and the night after, Jones canvassed more of the town without success. He was at the south side of Fifth Street when he turned the corner and saw a familiar face coming his way. It was Ellie, the waitress from Fiddle's Diner dressed in street clothes. She was carrying a sack of groceries with one hand and a six-pack of Ballantine in the other. He stepped into the circle of the street light and she stopped short, startled and then relaxed as she recognized Jones. "Well, if it isn't the King of the coal dock. What are you doing all the way up here, Mister Jones?"

"Taking in the night air, and getting to know the town a little better. Too busy working to walk around during the day." He pulled out his cigarettes and shook one out of the pack, offering it to her. "Smoke?"

"Thanks." She took the cigarette and Jones lit it for her then lit his own.

"Aren't you afraid to be out here walking by yourself? From what I've seen Brownsville's a pretty tough town."

She laughed and took a drag from her cigarette before saying, "I grew up on a farm with three brothers. Who worries? Besides, my room's right across the street and I can see old Mrs. Surovchak looking out the curtains at us. If anybody caused me a problem, she'd be on the phone to the cops in no time."

Jones nodded and Ellie said, "I'd invite you in for a beer, but Mrs. Surovchak has some strict rules about male visitors."

"Why don't you take your things inside and come back out and walk with me for a while?"

Ellie eyed Jones up and down. "I could do that. Wait here. I'll be right back."

Jones watched as she went into the house. In a moment, he saw a light in a second floor window that went out soon after. By the time he finished his second cigarette, Ellie was back. It was hard to tell under the street light, but to Jones, Ellie looked as if she had put on fresh lipstick. "So, let's take that walk—I don't want to just call you Jones—I mean, that's what I hear everybody call you, but it seems almost disrespectful. What does the C. O. stand for?"

"Two names I wish the orphanage never gave me."

Ellie was quiet for a moment then she nodded. "Okay, Jones it is. So, let's take a walk." She put her arm through his and they walked side by side down the sidewalk from one pool of light to the next.

"So, how long have you lived in Brownsville?"

"About four years. My husband Johnny grew up here then took a job in Kansas where we met. A couple of months after we got married his mother got sick and we came back here to take care of her. Then Johnny got drafted and he was killed on D-Day. My mother-in-law died the next year, but by then I had a job and I knew everybody here, so I stayed on. Where were you before you came to Brownsville?"

"Nowhere in particular," Jones said. "I got out of the Army after the war and I've traveled around a lot, working at whatever I could find. I even hitchhiked across the country all the way from Georgia to California."

"I'll bet you have some stories."

If you only knew, thought Jones. "A few," he said. "And I bet you've heard every one of them from every guy who served."

She laughed. "You'd win that one. Work in the diner, you hear them all."

As they walked through the warm darkness of the summer night, the small talk flowed, and as Jones fed Ellie the fiction about his current identity, he realized that it came more easily to him than the truth. It was easier to make up a life out of whole cloth. And less painful. And less dangerous for them both.

Jones felt no presence of magic as they strolled through the south side neighborhood. If anything, it seemed almost too normal. He heard snatches of conversation as they passed the houses; husbands and wives, mothers and daughters, old and young. The creak of a porch swing and the glow of a cigarette in the darkness of a tree lined street told him eyes watched as they passed but without threat or malice.

Jones and Ellie rounded a corner and Jones found himself on a brick way between a walled cemetery and what could loosely be described as a castle.

He ran a hand over a weathered stone. "Pretty old cemetery, huh?"

"It goes back to the 1700s," Ellie said. "And that's Cerullo's Funeral Home over there."

Jones laughed. "You're kidding. Right next door; that's really convenient, isn't it?"

Ellie laughed too. "I don't think so. This cemetery was full before the mortuary was ever built."

Jones pointed to the castle. "How about that place? I see it every day walking to work, but I've never heard anybody even mention it."

"That's because it was here long before anyone alive today. It's just part of the landscape if you live here. That's Bowman's Castle."

"Who'd build a castle in Brownsville?"

"Bowman." Ellie laughed at her own joke and at Jones's expression. "A man named Jacob Bowman set up a trading post here in the late seventeen hundreds. It was a good spot on the National Road, and on the river. He made a lot of money and left it to his son who built his own castle."

"I've seen castles in France and Germany. This place doesn't look so much like them. It's too squared off. And it's made of regular sized bricks instead of blocks of stone as big as bathtubs."

Ellie laughed. "Maybe he was showing the world that America had its own brand of royalty. Word is the place is haunted."

Jones took a few steps toward the building and stood still a moment. "No, I doubt it. But maybe that house below."

Ellie looked at him curiously. "Why would you say that?"

"Just a hunch."

"That house belonged to an old river captain. That gable in front was a lookout post where he could watch the river. I don't know about ghosts, though."

"But you know a lot about the history of this town, don't you?"

"I'm just curious the same as you are," she said. "So tell me about the castles in France and Germany."

CHAPTER TWENTY-SIX

Castles. *Tamno Mjesto,* "Dark Place" wasn't as elaborate as Nuschwanstein, nor as blunt and utilitarian as Augsburg. It was a heap of black stone atop a densely wooded mountain in the deep forest of Croatia. Torture extracted its location from a dying Nazi operative who told them, "I'd tell you to go to Hell, but instead, I tell you, go to *Tamno Mjesto.* I dare you."

Simmons and Hutz bivouacked on the next mountain, watching the castle for three days and planning their penetration. The place held no strategic advantage; rather its importance was concealment. For three days, the pair watched the only road in or out of the castle gate and for two of those days SS staff cars, sometimes alone, once in an arrogant parade, labored up the steep twisting path through the dark second growth pines. The third night as soon as an SS entourage rolled ceremoniously down the mountain road, Simmons and Hutz decided it was time to go in.

The pair had maintained radio silence for days, but before they entered the forest, Hennessey arranged to have an air strike on standby to destroy the place. "Find out what's in there, first, and if it's called for, we'll level the place, but not until we know whether there may be items of interest inside."

Items of interest: read occult weapons. "So you want us to just reconnoiter and see whether there's something in there worth stealing?" Hutz said. "And if there isn't, then the flyboys hit the place?"

"There's a little more to it than that," said Hennessey. "We also need to be sure that if we bomb the castle we don't upset any confinement measures and unleash something we don't know how to control. You of all people should be sensitive to that possibility." Hennessey's remark alluded to a Dresden crypt beneath the Frauenkirche Cathedral in which a pack of vampires had lain in coffins for more than a century. The infamous firebombing burned the stakes from their hearts and the crucifixes from their coffins, and the undead rose to terrorize an already beleaguered city. Although Simmons hadn't been there, Hutz was and barely escaped with his life.

So the mission was search and destroy, or maybe just a glorified burglary. Either way they were in place, the mission was set, and there was no turning back.

"I can only speak for me," said Hutz, "but I don't smell any magic in this place."

"Me either," said Simmons Both had come close to the massive pile of stone in the days before, but neither felt so much as a twinge. "But Hennessey says go, we go."

Hutz shrugged, slung his Sten over his shoulder and started down the mountain.

The dense tree cover that protected the castle from prying eyes also protected Simmons and Hutz from discovery as they worked their way through the dark forest. The outer walls on three sides of the castle were monolithic; the black stone facets rose from the ground as if something had broken through the roof of Hell. The fourth side offered an arched gateway with a half raised portcullis. Guards slouched at either side, four of them in all, their rifles leaning against the walls. They all wore the red fez of the Waffen division decorated with the skull and winged eagle of the SS.

From a quarter mile away Hutz studied the scene with binoculars then handed them to Simmons. "If Himmler saw those four so casual on duty, he'd have them all castrated with a sledgehammer. From the looks of the guards and their attitude, there may not be much of interest in the place. Maybe it's just a resort for storm troopers on leave."

"If that's what it is, why do they come and go in the same few hours?"

"You have a point, but if something really important is in there, they aren't taking drastic measures to guard it."

Maybe, thought Simmons, whatever's in there can take care of itself. "We still have to check it out. Intelligence says it's a hot spot, and they haven't been wrong yet." His thoughts drifted back to the dying officer's taunt: if you dare.

Intel told Hutz and Simmons that in the 14th century the Arpad dynasty, as a protection from the Muslim hordes that declared jihad on the Serbs and Croats, did as all prudent rulers do. They built escape routes for themselves into all of their palaces. This one had a tunnel that surfaced three hundred meters eastward in a nook between two mountain peaks.

Simmons had scouted the tunnel the night before and he found it unguarded and apparently without booby traps. It was overgrown with brush and small trees and if he didn't know it was there, he may not have found it at all. It was narrow but tall enough for men and horses to walk through upright in single file. Though the walls and earthen floor were moist, there were no stalactites. This was no water formation; the passage had likely been excavated by hand centuries before.

He and Hutz had gone approximately fifty meters into the dank, airless passage when they heard a flapping of hundreds of leathery wings. A flurry of bats swirled around them for a second then swarmed out into the night. He breathed easier when they flew away without attacking, as he recalled the Dresden vampires.

Another twenty meters brought them to a vertical iron grating made of welded steel bars set in a concrete base, a recent addition to the tunnel. "So that's why they don't have guards at the entrance," whispered Hutz. "More the fools they." The thought crossed Simmons's mind that maybe the bars were placed to keep something in, not out.

Hutz set his knapsack on the tunnel floor and pulled out a spool of what looked like grey twine in the dim light of Simmons's shielded lantern. He cut lengths of the cord and knotted them around the steel bars in a pattern roughly one meter square. "Goggles on," he whispered. Hutz struck a match and lit one of the knots. The thermite impregnated in the cord hissed and flared whitely as he lit the others in turn. The iron bars began to glow where the heat ate through them. Simmons and Hutz grabbed the grating with gloved hands, and as the white heat cut through the last bit of iron, they pulled the bars free, leaving an opening in the grate.

He set the smoking iron against the tunnel wall and pulled off his goggles. In the lantern light, he could see that the passage sloped upward and he couldn't see its end in the darkness. He climbed through the ragged opening in the grate and Hutz followed him, gun at the ready. In another hundred meters, the tunnel leveled off and curved to the right.

Simmons, taking point, raised a hand to halt. He shut one eye for a moment to acclimate it to darkness before closing the shield of the lantern and leaving them in total blackness. As their eyes adjusted a faint light glowed around the bend. He brought his arm down and he and Hutz crept through the tunnel toward the gradually brightening light.

Both of them caught a whiff of something strong cutting through the smell of damp earth, mold, and bat guano, something animal yet chemical at the same time. As they moved closer to the light, they heard voices, many voices muttering, growling indistinctly. They peered around the corner of the tunnel and saw a heavy door blocking the passage. Its lower half was thick timbers banded with iron and its upper half was heavily barred. It looked like original equipment. There was neither a knob nor hinges visible. Hutz pointed at it then gestured upward. It was likely raised by a winch and chain.

Hutz and Simmons slithered along the passage walls from either side to have a look through the bars into the room beyond. The ceiling was high, maybe twenty meters. The floor and walls were stone, the floor littered with mounds of straw and filth. Stone stairs had been removed, leaving the room a pit. Light came from torches in ancient iron wall sconces above. In the midst of this dank chamber, they saw a throng of naked human horrors.

They were men once but men no more. All were hypermuscular to the point in some cases of near disability. Some were so musclebound they couldn't raise their arms higher than their waists, arms whose hands had swollen and distorted into hooked claws. Their humped shoulders pushed heads forward until chins touched their bulging chests, and their eyes stared from the tops of their sockets.

And what eyes—reddish black like dark cherries, eyes that glared from beneath sloping foreheads, eyes that showed emptiness behind them; no intelligence, no will, no soul. The crowd of creatures milled about the chamber aimlessly, jostling, snorting, pissing, shitting like animals in a pen. In the flickering light, Simmons could make out numbers tattooed on the straining skin of their forearms. They were experiments.

"*Werwolfen*," Hutz whispered almost reverently.

As the Allies made deeper incursions into Europe and began moving into Germany itself, Goebbels devised a plan to terrorize invaders: he proposed a guerilla commando organization made up of the faithful to wreak havoc among the invading armies and among citizens through acts of such barbarous savagery as to demoralize the enemy and to frighten wavering locals into compliance by tales of monsters who carried out Hitler's orders. Hutz and Simmons had been briefed on the plan, but Hennessey imparted no inkling of how literally the SS intended to carry it forth.

There was no magic here, rather perverted Nazi science practiced on men willing to give not only their bodies but their souls for the Fatherland. Looking up, Simmons saw a rectangle of light, a platform with mechanism, and the silhouettes of men and of something larger. A voice rang out in a guttural language Simmons had never heard before, and the mass of man-things stopped shuffling and turned their heads as far upward as their bodies and their postures would allow. The voice spoke again, and the group backed away from the center of the room.

Simmons crouched to more easily see the doorway and realized the dark bulk was a steer. Docile, probably drugged, it was led onto the platform and a heavy sling passed under its belly. The sling was hooked to chains hanging overhead, and two men turned the windmill crank of a clanking winch. The steer was lifted from the platform and swung away. The gears ratcheted and slowly the steer was lowered into the room.

The creatures in the room stirred in anticipation, jostling each other to be in the forefront of their ungodly circle. The voice barked in that odd language again, and all of the beast men snapped to an odd kind of attention and remained still until the steer's hooves touched the floor. The voice barked a third command, and the creatures swarmed over the helpless beast, tearing chunks of its flesh from its bones and rending it with their teeth, eating it alive.

The helpless steer suddenly waking from its stupor bawled in pain and terror once, and then a maniacal claw ripped out its throat and it fell under the mass of swarming flesh.

Sickened at the sight and the thought of what a pack of these things would do to a civilian village or an unsuspecting patrol, Simmons turned away from the bars. He had seen more than enough. Even if this abomination were destroyed, the sight would haunt Simmons's nightmares for the rest of his life. He waved for Hutz to follow him, but Hutz remained, transfixed, fascinated by the gory spectacle. The Sight tingled, but before Simmons could stop him, Hutz barked an order in the bestial language, and the man-things froze. Silence fell.

"*Was ist loss?*" The voice shouted above. A quick command in German and another winch came into play, one that raised the door between Simmons and Hutz and the drooling horrors on the other side. Another command in the beast language needed no translation: Attack. The horde turned toward the lifting door and surged forward, claws groping for breathing meat.

Simmons grabbed Hutz and shoved him down the corridor. "Run, damn it! Run!"

Jarred from his trance, Hutz ran through the narrow passageway with Simmons close behind. Simmons turned and fired a spray of bullets into the chest of the leading monster. It kept coming unfazed. He lowered the Sten and fired, taking its legs off at the knees. The creature fell but kept crawling after them. "Legs!" he shouted at Hutz. "Shoot their legs."

Both Stens chattered and four more of the pursuers fell over each other, blocking the narrow tunnel. The bleeding barricade wouldn't last long, but it would buy them time. In a moment Hutz and Simmons clambered through the hole in the grate and reached the cave's opening only to be pinned down by gunfire. Two riflemen were firing tracer rounds from the wall high above.

"We have to get out of here fast before the guards from the gate make it around here and cut us off," Simmons said. "On three, you fire at the one to the left; I'll take the one to the right. One, two—" On three Hutz and Simmons bolted from the mouth of the tunnel. Simmons sprayed fire to the right and Hutz fired left. Simmons's target fell, and Hutz's sniper fired a round that missed Hutz but hit his knapsack.

The Sight showed Simmons the flare of the thermite cord an instant before it happened. He tried to pull Hutz's pack from his shoulder, but before he could the white flare blossomed like an evil flower, shooting under the flap of the knapsack, searing the side of Hutz's face and singeing Simmons's hand. Hutz screamed in agony. Simmons fired upward again and the second sniper tumbled from the aerie to land with a crackling of tree branches and a thrashing of brush. Simmons tossed a grenade into the tunnel as the first wave of the monster men neared the opening.

The grenade exploded with a sharp whump throwing the lead creature backward and collapsing the tunnel sealing the monsters inside it. Simmons heaved Hutz over his shoulder and ran.

They had at least a minute's start on the guards and before the probing lights could find them, Simmons had climbed into a hole he'd dug the day before, pulled Hutz in after him, and pulled the sod covered lid closed over them. In the hole, Simmons had hidden a field radio and a Morse key. He put on the headphones and dialed in the proper channel.

He was tapping the code for the air strike when Hutz woke. "What are you doing?" he said.

"Calling the strike," said Simmons.

"No!" cried Hutz, grabbing at the code key. "It's too valuable to destroy. We can learn how they did it and use it ourselves—fight fire with fire!"

Simmons hated to do it, but he punched Hutz full force on the good side of his jaw. *Can't risk being heard*, he thought. *Once the bombers hit the place, the guards will be too busy to look for us and I can get us out of here.*

Simmons finished the code. In seconds, confirmation came back. He switched off the radio and settled back in the dark, gun at the ready, to wait.

It was hours before Simmons heard the drone of the bombers and the distant crack of anti-aircraft fire. Twice the Waffen guards had walked right over their bolt-hole and not known it. He was thankful they didn't have dogs. Simmons took a large chance and injected Hutz, although he was in shock, with an ampoule of morphine to keep him sedated and to lessen his pain.

Once the bombing stopped, Simmons chanced leaving the covert. He scouted the area for a hundred meters around and, determining it safe,

"The grenade exploded…collapsing the tunnel…"

pulled Hutz from the hole and carried him back to their camp. It would be another thirty-six hours of cat and mouse before they would be taken by resistance fighters to the coast where they could be spirited away by ship. Lacking proper medical care, Hutz had become feverish from infection and even if he survived, his face was a ruin and he'd never do covert ops again.

CHAPTER TWENTY-SIX

"**W**hat?"

"Castles," said Ellie. "You were going to tell me about the castles you saw in Europe."

"Oh yeah, Europe's full of them. Seems like every good-sized town has one."

Jones and Ellie walked the quiet streets wrapped in the soft warmth of the summer night and the sound of crickets and music drifting from one window or another. At the sound of "Ain't Misbehavin'" Ellie started humming and turned gracefully, her right arm held up and out and her left across her chest. "So, Jones, you like music?"

"Who doesn't?"

"You like to dance?"

"Wish I knew how."

"I love it." She twirled, her skirt flaring out around her in the circle of a street lamp. "Johnny and I used to go all the time before he got drafted. We'd go to the Ivory Ballroom in Uniontown. Benny Goodman played there once. It was so packed we couldn't get in, so they opened the windows and the crowd danced on the sidewalk and in the streets. I miss that."

"Maybe I can learn."

Ellie stopped twirling. She looked him in the face and said, "Don't say that if you don't mean it."

"I wouldn't.'

Jones felt a tingle and the Sight showed him her lips reaching up to kiss him. He leaned forward and met her halfway. The kiss was warm and filled with promise. "That was a surprise," she said. "I thought I was kissing you."

Jones smiled in the darkness. "Sometimes smart people share a good idea."

Ellie put her arm through his and they walked a while longer, not talking now. When they got back to Ellie's boarding house, she slid her arm from his and said, "Well, Jones, it's been a pleasant time. I'd invite you in, but…"

"Mrs. Surovchak wouldn't understand."

"Right."

"There's always my place. We could take turns sleeping in the bed."

They both laughed and then her face got serious. "I don't think I'm ready for that yet, Jones. I don't really know what you do," she patted the automatic under his arm through his jacket, "but I know you do it for Skitch Mottolla. I already lost one man to a violent job. I don't know if I could stand to lose two."

Jones started to speak but Ellie put two fingers over his lips. "Not tonight, Jones." She kissed the tip of her index finger and touched it to the corner of his mouth. "Maybe soon."

Ellie turned and went into the house. Jones stood on the sidewalk until the light came on behind the upstairs window shade and until it went off again.

CHAPTER TWENTY-SEVEN

Two days later Jones had canvassed almost half of Brownsville's streets but still hadn't picked up any trace of magic. He was working the coal dock with another new guy, a big dark Irishman named O'Donnell. He was six inches taller than Jones and half again as broad across the shoulders and possessed of the attitude that size equals status. He didn't try to bully Jones; he'd been warned off that by Hankins. Instead he ran his mouth from the start of the shift to its end, laughing at his own bawdy jokes and answering his own questions when Jones didn't. "Am I right? Am I right?" he'd bellow about some half-baked opinion then follow the question with, "Damned straight I am."

Jones generally ignored O'Donnell and paid more attention to his shovel. Near the end of the shift, the yard engine shuttled a last coal car over the hopper. O'Donnell climbed the trestle and struck the trap lever with his hammer. The trap stayed closed, and O'Donnell struck it again with a loud clang.

Suddenly, Jones's tattoos began to twitch. His head swiveled from side to side. Nothing obvious in sight. O'Donnell cursed and hit the trap lever a third time as a low groan came from beneath the trestle. The Sight came and Jones saw the trestle collapsing toward him bringing the rail car with it. "O'Donnell, jump clear!" he shouted and instead of running away from the hopper, threw himself over the side into it as the trestle collapsed, tipping twenty-five tons of rail car and a hundred tons of coal into the dock.

The Irishman leapt from the trestle as it came down. He tried to run away from the falling rail car instead of toward it and was crushed like an ant under a giant boot. The bulk of the coal car fell beyond the hopper with a deep crash, spilling its load, but enough of the car's weight came to bear on the side of the hopper to bend the thick steel inward.

Inside the hopper Jones took a deep breath and immediately choked on the coal dust. The fallen rail car lay just inches overhead. He could almost reach out and touch its axles. At the far end of the hopper, Jones could see light and he crawled toward it, dragging himself over the sharp lumps of coal and fighting for air in the thick dust. He could hear men shouting and running. Twenty more feet. Ten. He felt the afternoon sun on his face. He shouted for help.

"My God! Someone's alive under there!" Jones pushed his head and shoulders over the steel rim of the hopper and gulped in air. Several pairs of hands seized his arms and dragged him out. Jones's head swam and the voices and noises fused into a red roar as he sank into darkness.

He came to a few minutes later to the acrid odor of smelling salts. He was outside, lying on his back on the concrete platform of the dock and looking up at a patch of blue sky. A group of the yard workers huddled over him. Jones tried to sit up and hands pushed him back down. "Just lie still," a voice said. "The ambulance is on the way."

"O'Donnell; what about O'Donnell?" Jones croaked.

"We haven't gotten to him yet." It was Hankins. "When we do there won't be much to him. He's under the car."

Jones turned his head. The beams of the trestle were twisted like taffy. "Damndest thing I ever saw," said Hankins quietly. "There was no reason for it to let go." Jones saw the coal car lying on its side, its load half in and half out, fanned across the dock. Like a spilled pot of black rice, Jones thought. Like a spilled chest of onyx beads.

CHAPTER TWENTY-EIGHT

Onyx beads – a curtain of them separated the front of the little basement shop from the back, and through them Simmons could see shelves of flasks, urns, and dusty boxes. The London apothecary shop traded in modern medicines but these shared space with bins of exotic roots and hanging bundles of dried flowers and plant stalks. On the counter, leeches swam in a large glass ginger jar.

Simmons's tattoos began to itch as soon as he stepped down from the sidewalk and through the door. A spring bell announced his entry, but no one appeared immediately, giving him a chance to look the place over. The Japs were still fighting hard in the Pacific theater but Germany was nearing collapse. Hitler's use of magic had shifted from conquest to revenge. Like Milton's Satan, he would destroy what he could not rule. Intel determined that pockets of wizardry were springing up in allied countries to wreak havoc on the home front and to weaken the resolve of their people; one last serpent to be scotched.

The onyx beads parted and a short, squat man passed from the back room to the counter. As he approached, Simmons's tattoos began to throb. The magic was strong in this one. The bald man was dressed in a rusty black suit, a yellowed dress shirt missing its celluloid collar, and thick lensed glasses that made his black eyes frog-like. He wore grey gloves on his hands; the left forefinger had worn through, and Simmons saw a dark fingernail hooked like a talon pushing through the opening.

"Yessssss?" The shopkeeper's voice drew out the sibilance. "How may I help you?" His accent was unplaceable. The voice should have been inaudible, but Simmons felt as well as heard every syllable, as if the man were speaking inside his head. He smiled, and Simmons saw teeth not pointed, but angular like fangs whose points had been filed off. Their appearance was just enough to give the impression of a feral predator.

Simmons pulled a list from his pocket and said, "I need several items that I can't find elsewhere. Perhaps you have them here."

"We have many things you may not find elsewhere," the shopkeeper said. "May I see your list?"

"Yes, these things." He held out the list to hand it to the shopkeeper. The little man's hand flashed across the counter like a sprung trap and seized Simmons's wrist in a crushing grip. He turned Simmons's hand over, revealing the runes on the back side of the paper.

"You are a fool to think me one," he said, grinning wickedly. "You'll not pass those runes to me, human." Simmons's hand lashed out and his fist smashed into the thick glasses, pushing the twisted wire frame into one of those round black eyes. The shopkeeper roared in pain but didn't slacken his grip on Simmons's wrist. His mouth opened wide and Simmons saw a second set of ripsaw teeth hidden behind the first. The shopkeeper was a troll.

The creature slammed Simmons's forearm to the counter and laughed, a hollow, echoing sound from deep in its chest. Simmons could feel the bones in his wrist grinding. The troll stretched the fingers of its free hand and nails popped through the glove like cat's claws. It swiped at Simmons's face but missed, its reach impaired by its height and the counter between them. Simmons flicked his free wrist and a silver knife dropped into his palm. He slashed it at the shopkeeper's face and when the creature pulled back from the silver and the runes carved in the blade, Simmons drove it full force through the enemy's forearm pinning it to the counter.

This time, the troll screamed as foul green smoke poured from the wound but still held his grip on Simmons's wrist. "I'll eat your heart," it hissed, snapping at Simmons's face. The troll caught Simmons's free arm and dragged him half over the counter. Fangs bit deep, snapping ribs and tearing flesh. Simmons could feel the burn of venom in his side. Then the troll's head snapped back and choking, it spat a gobbet of Simmons's skin from its maw. The glowing tattoo was poison to the troll.

The troll threw back its head roaring, its tongue on fire, and from behind it, a bright blade flashed and the creature's head tumbled from its shoulders and rolled into a corner where it landed upright. For a few seconds a hateful light flashed from its remaining eye, then went out like a snuffed candle.

Simmons saw his MI-5 counterpart Guinness wiping the blade of a hooked Ghurkha knife on the troll's suit. His face, sandy hair, and moustache were spotted with dark blood. Guinness looked at the troll's hand, locked in a death grip around Simmons's wrist and with a short chop severed it from the creature's forearm. Simmons, nearly unconscious from shock and pain tumbled backward onto the floor. Guinness vaulted the counter and hauled him to his feet. "Sorry to be late for the party, mate. You should have seen what I had to fight to get through the back door."

Simmons felt as if the floor were tilting and whirling. Guinness put a shoulder under Simmons's arm and said, "We've got to get out of here now. We'll pry that claw off you later."

"Wait," said Simmons weakly. "Tattoo." He pointed to the gob of skin and flesh the troll had bitten from him.

Without letting go of Simmons, Guinness scooped the red mass from the floor and thrust it in his pocket. "Now, my friend, we have to get out of here, because in a minute or so there'll be no here left."

Guinness dragged Simmons around the counter and through a storeroom where something indescribable lay in a tattered heap of flesh and bone. In the alley, Guinness propped Simmons against a wall and signaled with his flashlight. A car started up the block and rolled toward them lights off. Guinness pulled the back door of the sedan open and shoved Simmons inside. "Take him to base. He's hurt bad and needs special attention."

Simmons grabbed Guinness's coat and croaked again, "Tattoo."

"Oh bloody hell." Guinness took the bitten flesh from his pocket and thrust it into Simmons's hand. "If I were you, I'd get that sewn back on, mate," he said, closing the car door. "Never know when it might come in handy again, right?"

As the sedan turned the corner, Simmons heard the explosion, but his eyes were closed too tightly by his pain to see the flash.

CHAPTER TWENTY-NINE

Over his protests the roundhouse workers loaded Jones into a car and hauled him to the hospital. Various parts of him hurt to various degrees, but the worst damage to him was the black dust in his lungs. He figured he'd be coughing up coal for the next six months.

After considerable poking and prodding, the emergency room doctor pronounced Jones fit to leave and when he walked out of the hospital, Danny Hayes was leaning on his rusted Pontiac smoking a Camel. "So, Jones," he said, "Ready for a good job now?"

CHAPTER THIRTY

The next day, Jones ate breakfast late because he wasn't going to the coal dock. He walked into a nearly empty Fiddle's with his newspaper under his arm. Ellie looked up from the counter and stared unspeaking. Jones smiled and slid into a booth. "Good morning."

Ellie snapped, "That's all you have to say, Jones? Good morning?" She slammed a plate on the counter and Jones was surprised it didn't break. "How can you sit there and think about breakfast? You damn near died yesterday."

"But I didn't. And even if I died this afternoon, I still have to eat breakfast this morning."

Ellie brought a cup and the coffee pot. She shook her head. "When I said 'violent job,' the coal dock wasn't what I had in mind."

"I guess I'm like a cat. Nine lives and I still have a few left. Anyway, I won't be working there anymore. So, how about ham and eggs and some home fries?"

CHAPTER THIRTY-ONE

The first few days on Skitch's payroll were uneventful. Jones spent a good part of it shooting pool and working out in the gym now that he didn't have the coal dock to keep him in shape.

He was working the heavy bag when he saw everybody run to the windows to look down onto the street. He stopped his routine and joined them to see what was happening. Two floors below across the street, a big man in a work jacket was beating the hell out of one of the town cops. An older woman in a flowered dress, probably his mother, but who knew for sure, cheered him on. "That's Tommy Shotter pounding Mike Gavin," said one of the guys. "Looks like Gavin's getting the worst of it."

Gavin was on the ground now, and the man was kicking him in any available location. At that moment, Danny Hayes and two more of Skitch's men came running out of the poolroom across the street. "This ought to be good," said another of the gym rats. As Skitch's men crossed the street the old woman stooped over Gavin and pulled his service revolver from its holster and raised it at the men. "Stay back, boys," she said, cocking the hammer. Skitch's men stopped in mid-stride and began to retreat. Meanwhile, her son was pounding Gavin's head on the sidewalk. People on the street has stopped to watch the fun, but at the sight of the gun retreated into the shops and storefronts to watch from cover.

Like a blonde panther Hayes ran up the running board and over the fender of a parked car and dove through the air, tackling the woman and taking the pistol from her. The other two grabbed the beater and slammed him face up over the hood of a car. Jones saw the glint of a straight razor at Shotter's eye.

Danny looked up past the gym windows to the fourth floor. He nodded at some order Jones couldn't hear and jerked his head to the side saying, "Take him in the alley." At that moment, the old woman screeched and ran at Danny, her fingers hooked into claws planning to tear out his eyes. Danny casually backhanded her across the forehead with the pistol and she fell like a bag of laundry, sprawled on the sidewalk.

He lifted Gavin to his feet and put his revolver back in the holster. Danny held the cop upright as he walked unsteadily across the street to the poolroom. Jones figured that justice, however rude, was being dispensed around the corner. The show over, the men in the gym went back to their weights and punching bags. Not my business, thought Jones, but a curiosity just the same.

Later that evening, sitting on a stool at the Red Feather, he asked Danny, "I saw the fight out front today. What was that all about?"

"Gavin shot the old woman's dog. Gavin said it was rabid. She said it wasn't rabid, just cranky from the heat. She must have been brushing its teeth because Gavin said he saw foam in its mouth."

"Maybe I shouldn't ask, but why did you guys jump in?"

Danny took a pull from his beer and sat silent for a moment, as if deciding how deep to go answering the question. "This town runs pretty smooth for us, for the cops, for everybody. People here know they can walk down the street and they won't get mugged, raped, murdered. And it's not because the bad guys are afraid of the cops. They're afraid of what we'll do to keep order, but some days tempers get the best of common sense, and..." He shrugged and went on.

"As long as things are running on an even keel, the cops just walk their beats and have it easy. The less they have to fight, the better, and they aren't too interested in looking under the ice to see what's in the river or wondering how it got there."

"The path of least resistance."

"The what?"

"It's like water. It flows the easiest course and gradually wears a channel for itself to follow."

"Don't get me wrong; we have plenty of tough cops here, but they know they have a better time when we keep a hand on the town too. As for saving Gavin's ass today, I think of it as a professional courtesy. That and a favor owed."

Jones nodded and held up his fingers for two more beers. "Sounds like a good arrangement."

Danny nodded. "I grew up here. It's been that way as long as I can remember."

"One other thing I'm curious about, Danny," said Jones. Everybody else on Skitch's crew has a last name ends in a vowel. How'd a blond Mick with the last name of Hayes ever get on board?"

Danny laughed. "My grandmother, rest her soul, was a Calabrese. I guess Skitch figured one quarter Dago and three-quarters Marine qualified me."

Jones tipped his bottle to Danny. "I'll drink to that logic."

Danny finished his beer and stood up. "So, Jones, a bunch of us are going to Aunt Willa's for some laughs. Want to come along?"

"Aunt Willa's?"

"The local cat house. It ain't the Moulin Rouge, but it keeps Brownsville smiling."

Jones shook his head. "Maybe next time. I have things to do tonight."

"Okay, pal, but you don't know what you're missing. Nothing takes the edge off like a good run at a whorehouse."

CHAPTER THRITY-TWO

Whorehouse.

Brothel.

Cologne.

Simmons stayed in the shadows, his collar turned up against the cold persistent drizzle. Ahead, Simmons's target Simon LeClerq, thief, dealer in occult objects, and Nazi collaborator ambled leisurely along the twisting street.

Simmons had followed the portly Frenchman for the better part of the last few days, waiting for an opportunity to take him out of the game. LeClerq was no wizard himself, but he knew where to find them and made a tidy profit procuring occult artifacts for the Third Reich. Surveillance uncovered a network of contacts to be dispatched, all in the same hour by the team in a grand sweep. Simmons drew LaClerq.

He followed the fat fence most of the afternoon and into the evening, keeping him in sight until the appointed time. LaClerq visited his bank where he withdrew a thick wad of banknotes then went to his barber for a haircut and a shave, browsed a bookstall, and patronized a restaurant where the glutton ordered Chateaubriand for two and devoured both portions, washing them down with two bottles of wine. Now he was on the street in Cologne's red light district.

LeClerq turned into a gateway and strode across a courtyard to the front door of a stately but seedy town house. A fountain bubbled water over cherubs and a beatific Venus bathed in the subtle colors of light through a stained glass window. He rapped at the door with its lion's head knocker and in a moment, a woman in an elegant dress opened the door. LeClerq was invited inside immediately. Simmons crossed two more streets before turning a corner and doubling back toward the alley at the rear of the block. He put his head down and shuffled as if he were drunk.

The alley was empty except for a tall, lean man slouched at the gate of the town house's back yard. Whatever was inside the house, it was important enough to be guarded. As he passed the man, a two-inch steel ball on a braided cable dropped from Simmons's sleeve.

Simmons spun on his heel whipping the cable around his head once for momentum and connected with the guard's temple. The guard fell without a sound.

Simmons dragged the unconscious guard inside the wall and across the narrow yard to the back of the house. A quick search of the man's pockets produced a ring of keys. Simmons tried the keys and the third one opened the door onto a darkened pantry. Piano music came from another part of the town house, a complex classical piece Simmons couldn't place. The pantry shelves were empty. Simmons ran a finger over one of them and found a film of dust. This was no residence.

He crossed the kitchen and eased down the hallway toward the sound of music. He passed a darkened dining room and peered around the edge of the doorway into an elegant parlor with a fire roaring in a huge fireplace. The woman who had answered the door sat alone at a grand piano, her back to the doorway. A wad of banknotes sat beside her on the bench. LeClerq must be upstairs.

Simmons slipped back into the kitchen where he had seen servant's stairs leading to the upper floors. The old treads creaked, and Simmons was grateful for the piano music. The second floor was another testimony to the house's grandeur. A crystal chandelier threw myriad tiny rainbows on the papered walls and thick wine-red carpet.

Simmons put his ear to the first door. No sound. The second and third doors yielded the same result. Behind the fourth door, Simmons heard the murmurs and moans of passion. He silently turned the knob and opened the door an inch to look inside.

A huge four-poster bed covered in black satin sheets dominated the room, and on it, in the flickering light of candles, Simmons found LeClerq. The naked Frenchman's obscenely fat body was spread-eagled face up, his hands and feet tied to the bedposts with braided scarlet cords. The black satin sheets contrasted the fish-belly white of his flabby thighs and gross stomach.

Simmons' tattoos twitched. Three of the most beautiful women Simmons had ever seen slithered over the Frenchman, rubbing their naked flesh against his disgusting rolls of fat. As Simmons watched, one of the women gaped her mouth wide, showing fangs that she buried in LaClerq's thigh. Vampires. No brothel fantasy; these creatures were real. LaClerq cried out in ecstasy, as a second bit into his wrist, feeding on the blood that oozed from the wound. The third gently closed her lips on the groaning man's throat.

LaClerq's eyes rolled back in his head as the throes of ecstasy overtook him and he writhed in slow motion on the blood-slicked sheets. Well, thought Simmons, at least he'll die happy.

He drew his pistol; its barrel extended by a suppressor and pointed it through the doorway. Simmons's aim was good. He fired two shots, phut-phut, one into each of LaClerq's unseeing eyes.

The vampires hissed in anger, their treat of living blood interrupted. The women rose from the bed and stalked toward the door, their moves sinuous and feral. The piano played louder and faster, the concerto's movement intensifying. Simmons had to fight the mesmerizing gaze of the temptresses as they emerged from the doorway, the chandelier's tiny rainbows dappling their flawless skin.

He grabbed his cuff and tore it back, revealing the crucifix tattooed on his wrist. The vampires shrank from the icon, and Simmons advanced, forcing them to retreat into LaClerq's chamber. The Sight tingled. Behind him. A door opened and Simmons dodged quickly enough that a swinging truncheon missed the back of his head and instead caught him on the shoulders and drove him to his hands and knees. The pistol fell to the carpet.

Simmons rolled away from a second blow from the club wielded by a burly man in a dark suit. The blow glanced off his upper arm, and

Simmons's foot shot out in a mule kick, catching the thug in the groin. He dropped the club and doubled over in pain. The vampires were coming back into the hallway.

Simmons thought quickly and dealt with both problems at once. He leapt to his feet and grabbed the man by the hair, pulling his head back and exposing his throat. One quick slash with his knife and his attacker's blood spurted in jets.

Simmons shoved the bleeding man at the vampires, and the women's lust for blood overcame their anger. They fell upon him in a pack, greedily drawing his life from his veins. They were between Simmons and the back stairs, so he had no choice. He ran headlong down the grand staircase toward the frantic sound of the jangling piano.

Simmons had almost reached the parlor doorway when he was tackled by the guard he'd knocked out outside. The pair rolled through the doorway, locked in a mortal struggle. The piano ceased. The woman screamed and jumped to her feet, upsetting the bench.

The pair rolled toward the fireplace. The guard had his hands on Simmons's throat and was pushing his head toward the flames. Simmons felt the heat singeing his hair. He jammed his thumbs into his attacker's eyes and forced him back, rolling away from the hearth.

The guard grabbed a poker from the fireplace and charged with a roar. Simmons dropped his shoulder and got under the headlong rush, lifting his attacker from the floor and using his momentum to heave him into the open grand piano with a dissonant clang of strings as the lid slammed shut over him.

The woman rushed at him, screaming in French, and clawed at his face with her dark nails. One left to her jaw and she fell to the carpet.

Simmons dashed through the front door and turned as he passed the fountain, pulling the pin on a phosphorous grenade. The grenade sailed through the stained glass, and in a moment, flames shot through every window, but Simmons couldn't see them. He was already two blocks away running for the safe house.

CHAPTER THIRTY-THREE

Just like the Army, much of his job with Skitch was time spent waiting for orders. For Skitch, most of those involved little more than being an intimidating presence, going with a bagman to let people see who would come back alone if they didn't cooperate. When he tired of shooting pool, Jones sat on the bench across the street from the poolroom and read to pass the time. The Friday after the coal dock accident Jones was sitting on the bench when Danny sprawled beside him and lit a cigarette. "So, Jones, what are you reading?"

"Dashiel Hammet: *The Maltese Falcon.*"

"Oh yeah? They showed us that movie when we were in Guam. We liked it so much we made them run it again. That Sam Spade—he's my kind of hero. Tough, cool, smart, a good dresser, and he didn't let the dame get her hooks in him."

"Yeah, but that's Bogart and that's Hollywood," said Jones. "Real people have to earn those stripes the hard way."

"Like you and me, huh?"

"I guess so."

Across the street, the grocer, a small bald man in a blood stained butcher's apron was arranging produce in the sidewalk bins in front of his store. Danny pointed to him and said, "Could you imagine Sam Spade doing that job? Or selling shoes?" Danny affected a bad Bogart imitation: "Yesh, ma'am, I think we have thosh pumps in a nine triple-E. Let me check in the shtoreroom." Danny snorted. "If I had to do that all day, I'd go nuts in a week. But then again, I guess those shoe salesmen get to eyeball a lot of gams, huh?"

"Every job has its upside."

"Hey, Jones," Bucky shouted from the poolroom door. "Skitch wants to see you. He said to send you right up."

"Duty calls." Jones stood, tucked his book in the pocket of his jacket and waded through the traffic across the street. He climbed the stairs behind Bucky to the second floor and crossed the gym to the elevator. Skitch's driver Jerry opened the cage and gestured for him to step inside. The elevator passed the third floor and the cage opened on the fourth to a flurry of activity in the wire room.

People were running back and forth from table to table organizing the policy slips in advance of the close of the U. S. Treasury Department for the day and the publication of their daily balance. The last three numbers of the balance, a number all but impossible to rig, determined the winners. In the meantime, the boss of the wire room, Richie Traficante was on two or three of the phones on his desk at a time fielding bets while he watched with one eye the tote board for race results from Pimlico. Jones crossed the floor weaving through the tables and knocked on Skitch's door.

"Come in." Skitch was leaning back in his chair with a cigarette in his mouth, his shiny shoes on his desk and his hands behind his head. He waved to a chair. "Sit down, Jones. Take a load off."

"Bucky said you wanted to see me."

"I need you to do something tonight."

"What's the job?"

"It's a pretty simple deal. You ever hear of New Kensington?" Skitch said.

"Little Chicago? Yeah. I've heard about it once or twice."

"Got a call from one of the New Ken boys. Seems one of the Cleveland families has to make some sort of – call it restitution – payment to New Kensington. I didn't ask why and I don't want to know. We're going to middleman between the two, take the cash from the Cleveland boys and deliver it to New Ken to avoid confrontation between the two parties."

"We're going to Cleveland?" said Jones.

Skitch shook his head. "Cleveland's coming to us. You know Vic Menge. He's my regular bagman. Vic knows the score. He'll handle the pickup. You ride shotgun. Vic runs his normal schedule. The Cleveland boys hand the cash off to Vic and he bags it as if it's part of the regular take. People see Vic doing what he always does, nobody thinks twice. Just looks like the same old same old. If we keep it quiet, nobody's the wiser and we don't have any problems. In the meantime, you're in a car behind him just in case."

"Just me?"

"If I send an army, it'll tip people off that something's up. Besides, everybody around knows all my boys. You're a new face."

"I can see the dodge working," Jones said. "Where do we deliver the money?"

"You bring it here. It's only four or five miles away. Once it's here it's as safe as the bank. Then New Ken sends their boys to pick it up."

"Seems complicated. Why don't the Cleveland boys just bring it here?"

"Because word gets around. The fewer dots the Feds connect between us and them, the better for everybody."

"And if things go south?"

"That's why I'm sending you, Jones. You'll do what you have to do. Be back here around eight o'clock."

Jones skipped his workout and went back to his room to get ready. At eight he was riding the elevator back to the fourth floor. When he walked into Skitch's office, Vic Menge was sitting in a chair talking with Skitch. Menge looked as if he were going night clubbing dressed in a light weight

"Jones…waded through the traffic…"

tan suit with a navy blue shirt, a loud wide necktie, and two-toned shoes. His black hair was slicked back with a razor sharp part and his thin mustache looked as if someone had painted it on his lip with a grease pencil.

For the night's work, Jones wore a loose jacket over khaki slacks and a dark sport shirt. Under the jacket he carried his .45 automatic in a shoulder rig, and the Sten gun minus the stock and suppressor would ride on a rawhide thong under his right arm so that he could quickly swing it up and fire it if necessary. Because the clip stuck out at a tough angle to hide, he carried the Sten empty and kept a full clip in each of his jacket pockets.

Skitch went over the plan again. Vic would drive his own car and go in alone as he usually did to make his pickups maintaining the pretense that it was all business as usual. Jones would tail Vic in the Ford through the whole route. The last pickup would be the big one, and Jones would be there to watch the transfer and follow Vic back to Brownsville in case there was trouble.

"I don't get why Jones here has to follow me around all night. Can't he just meet me at the big stop?"

"Jones is riding along just in case tonight's the one night in a thousand some *strunz* gets ambitious and tries to knock you over for the small change. I can't risk anything fouling up this deal. The situation's too delicate."

"Nothing to it," Vic said. "I just make my regular stops and nobody sees anything different. I don't see why I need a nursemaid, Skitch."

"Better safe than sorry," Skitch said. "Right, Jones?"

Jones shrugged. "You're the boss."

"Well then," said Vic, putting on his hat as he stood, "let's start the show."

The evening was uneventful as Jones followed Vic from one seedy place to another, watching from his car as Vic went into grocery stores, poolrooms, brothels, and bars picking up envelopes of cash. At a ramshackle speakeasy down the river in Roscoe, Vic came out and instead of getting into his yellow Oldsmobile came over to Jones's car. "Next stop, the big one, Jones."

Vic pulled away from the curb and Jones followed his taillights to the highway and into the night.

Jones had passed the High Point a few times coming and going; it was the road house equivalent of a shotgun shack. The dirty white clapboard building perched on the edge of a steep hillside that plummeted almost three hundred feet to a horseshoe bend in the Mon River below. The two hundred seventy degree turn was called the Hell Stretch by river men for more than a century because it was so tough to navigate with a string of barges in tow.

The parking spaces in front of the roadhouse were filled and Vic and Jones had to park across the road in a gravel lot. Jones pulled his coupe into the lot behind Vic's Oldsmobile and found a space three spots over beside a pickup truck with a canopy that read Wilson Plumbing over the bed. He backed his car into the space so that it faced the road. Seconds saved in a getaway; old habits die hard, he thought. Jones let Vic cross the road first and go inside alone. Better that no one see them walk in together. The High Point's windows were open and the sounds of music and laughter drifted through them into the hot summer night.

He crossed the road and pushed open the double doors at the middle of the building. To the left Jones saw a bar lined with stools that stretched to the kitchen area at the far end. To the right ranks of booths lined either wall, the room ending at a small dance floor and a low cramped stage. Windows at every booth gave the interior the look of an oversized dining car.

Somebody had painted a blue sky and clouds on the ceiling years before, but decades of cigarette smoke and the dim lighting gave it a yellow cast you might see before a tornado. On the stage an accordionist and a trumpet player were wrestling with "Sentimental Journey" and a handful of couples were on the dance floor wrestling with each other. The crowd looked like working stiffs in last season's clothes, dressed in their best but still looking shabby. The women seemed to be trying too hard because they knew they had to. Jones caught himself betting that Ellie had never seen the inside of the place.

Vic slid into a booth opposite two other men. Jones followed a few seconds later. One of the men was old and one was young. The young one puffed at a cigarette and the old one chewed the unlit stub of a cigar. Both were swarthy and sported the same long straight nose. "Gino, this is C. O. Jones, part of the crew," Vic said over the music. "Jones, this is Gino Scalise; he owns this fine establishment. And this is his son Gino junior."

"Sonny," the younger Scalise said with a nod.

Gino waved the waitress over. She was a cute little woman until she smiled and you saw her teeth. "Ginny," he said. "Bring us another round and get these guys whatever they want."

Vic leered. "You know what I want, Ginny." He put his hand on her arm. She shook it off with a laugh and said. "I know what you always want, Vic. You'll take a boilermaker and like it." She turned to Jones. "And you?"

"Same for me." "Sentimental Journey" ended to modest applause and the musicians took a stab at "Georgia on my Mind."

"Business good tonight?" Vic swiveled his head to look over the crowd.

"Naah," said Gino. "These bums come in here, buy one beer, drop anchor, and hope they get lucky. I oughta change the sign and just call it an amateur whore house. I'd make better money."

Vic was busy watching the women. Jones was busy watching the men, eyes open for anyone who looked out of place, looked edgy, or affected the practiced nonchalance of professional predators. He Said to Gino, "Over my shoulder; tall guy in a black shirt and a red necktie. He's carrying under his jacket. Left armpit. One of yours?"

"You got a good eye," said Sonny. "That's Chazz. He's Dad's driver."

"See anybody here tonight doesn't belong?"

"Nope, just the regulars."

Vic laughed. "Relax, Jones. Drink up. This is a cakewalk, just business as usual."

Jones nodded but his eyes kept scanning the crowd. In his experience business as usual made people lazy and careless. Vic wasn't taking this seriously, and that could be a costly mistake, tonight or the next time or the next time.

Two songs later, Chazz came to the booth and leaned over to say something in Sonny's ear. Sonny nodded and said to Jones and Vic, "The package is ready. Come with me."

They got up and followed Chazz and Sonny past the bar and through the kitchen into a store room where a man wearing gold rimmed glasses and a silk suit that cost as much as a new Buick sat at a scarred table. He looked as out of place in the grimy storeroom as a linen napkin in a coal bin and obviously wasn't happy to be in the dump. Maybe eating crow is part of the payoff, Jones thought. Behind the table a pair of hardcases with cheaper suits but bigger biceps stood guard. One of them set a steel box painted to look like a briefcase on the table and opened its hinged lid. The box was full of banded twenties.

Vic pulled a random bundle of bills from the case, zipped his thumb over it and nodded. "All green" he said with a grin. The suit didn't laugh or even crack a smile. Neither did his bodyguards. Vic replaced the bundle, closed the case and reached into his pocket. He put a heavy padlock through the hasp and snapped it shut. "Only the boss has the key," he explained to Jones. "Bring the case, would you, Sonny." He turned to the visitors and tipped his hat. "Thank you, gentlemen. Pleasure to do business with you. See you next time. And if you're staying for dinner, I recommend the beef bourguignon." Like poking at a lion through the bars of his cage, thought Jones.

"You cheap punk..." One of the big guys behind the table started forward. Jones reached into his jacket, but the man in the glasses put up a hand. The bodyguard froze. The Cleveland boss clenched his jaw. His eyes burned into Vic's and Jones hoped for Vic's sake those two never met again.

"Come on," said Sonny. "We'll go out the back." Chazz stepped out first, watchful, his gun down at his side. He looked in every direction then said. "Looks clear."

Before Jones stepped outside, he took his automatic from the rig and thumbed back the hammer. If somebody was going to make a try at the money, this was a likely time to do it while they were in the open. Vic was playing this all too casually for what was at stake. He followed Sonny, Chazz, and Vic through the cars in front toward the road.

"My car is right over there," said Vic, stepping ahead of Sonny and Chazz. At the edge of the road Vic stopped to put a cigarette in his mouth. He pulled out his lighter and flicked it once, twice, three times. Jones felt the Sight tingle. He saw it coming.

It all happened at once. At the end of the parking lot an engine roared into life and headlights came on. Chazz and Sonny whirled toward the sound and Vic pulled his revolver. Chazz was closer, so Vic put a bullet through the side of his head first then shot Sonny in the chest. As he turned his gun on Jones, Jones was already pulling the trigger. Vic was dead before he hit the ground, a slug through the center of his forehead.

In the meantime, the car, a dark green Hudson Commodore slid to a stop and men with guns poured out of all its doors. Caught in the open, Jones scooped up the case and held it in front of him as a shield. Bullets punched through the steel and one grazed his knuckles as he dove into the parked cars. He fired back with the automatic then shoved it into his waistband. He dropped the case and slapped a clip into the Sten. Jones popped up behind a Buick touring car and fired three quick bursts at his attackers. One of the five went down. He emptied the rest of the clip into the Hudson, hoping he hit something vital.

One of the four remaining gunmen stayed behind the car, a tall guy wearing a snap brim cap and firing an M-1 rifle. He meant to keep Jones pinned down while the others went to his right behind the cars in the lot. Jones slammed his second clip into the Sten and rolled under a flatbed truck, pushing the bullet-pocked case through the gravel ahead of him. Above him, slugs whined off fenders and shattered windshields, showering him with broken glass.

Two cars away Jones saw a pair of feet. He fired a burst from the machine gun under the cars and heard a scream. A dark shape landed where the feet had been and he fired another burst into it. Seven cars still stood between him and his coupe. At least one of the remaining hit men had a clear shot at him from behind the Hudson, plus the driver who was firing from inside the car. Jones jumped up and let loose with the Sten, blowing windows out of the Hudson and forcing the gunman behind it and the driver to duck as Jones sprinted for his coupe, letting the empty Sten swing by its lanyard as he pulled his automatic.

By this time, people inside the High Point were screaming. Jones felt the jolt as a bullet grazed his shoulder and he almost dropped the case. He spun and fanned half a dozen shots of cover fire. The doors of the High Point burst open and the bodyguards from the back room ran out, guns blazing. One of the gunmen from the Hudson popped up with a shotgun and fired at the new targets, putting one of the big guys on the ground. Jones fired a three-shot triangle into shotgun's chest. Three down. Time to go.

Jones yanked the door of his coupe open as a bullet ricocheted off the roof of the plumbing truck beside him. The other bodyguard wasn't taking sides; he was shooting at anybody with a gun. Jones fired back a spray of shots over his head to drive him to cover and threw the case onto the seat. The Ford rumbled into life and the tires sprayed gravel as he roared onto the highway.

Behind him the robbers jumped into the Hudson and the chase was on.

Jones thumbed the catch of the automatic and dropped the clip. It was empty. One round left in the chamber. He ran a stop sign, cutting off another car with a screech of brakes and a blaring horn and wheeled left onto another blacktopped road. If he could only pull over for a minute and get the shotgun from the trunk he'd have a better chance, but a look in the mirror told him the lights behind were closing. Coakee's words came back to Jones: You'll have to out drive him.

CHAPTER THIRTY-FOUR

The Ford was a pretty fast car. Coakee's modifications to the flathead V-8 made it tough to catch on a straightaway, but the twisting country road made speed less the issue in this contest than weight. The Hudson wasn't exactly a Gran Prix machine, but the chassis was low slung and it had a powerful inline 8. Jones's biggest worry was that the driver was an ace, and in a collision, the Ford would come out second. Tires squealed as Jones whipped through a tight S-curve and roared down a short straightaway.

The road swung left into the woods and Jones found himself in a narrow corridor with rough pavement, shallow berms, and thick pines close by on either side. No place to duck and cover. No way out but straight ahead.

Somebody had done a good setup on the Hudson too. It came up fast and Jones braced himself for an impact that never came. The Commodore's front bumper gently touched the left side of the Ford's and the driver cracked the gas and cut his wheel, trying to use the Hudson's weight and power to push the lighter Ford into a spin. Jones saw it coming and twitched the wheel, slipping past the maneuver before he was run off the road.

The Hudson swung into the passing lane then jogged to the right, clipping the Ford's reinforced bumper and knocking its back end almost off the pavement. Jones fought the wheel to straighten it out and floored the gas, pulling away. A bullet spidered the rear windshield. At least they weren't using a shotgun.

In the side mirror, Jones saw one of the gunmen lean out the rear passenger window, angling for a better shot. The next bullet blew out the back glass completely and punched through the windshield. A shard of glass sliced his right cheek and Jones could feel hot blood running down his jaw into his collar. Ahead, he saw the long X of a railroad crossing sign. "Come on, honey," Jones said to the Ford. "As you love me."

The Ford hit the high hump at seventy, the front bumper dragging, and the car was airborne like a skier on a jump. Jones felt a tingling in his brain. The Sight showed him that the crossing was a double. He stood on the brakes with the coupe in the air and when the Ford landed with a shriek of rubber, the Hudson bottomed out and rocketed ahead, nosing into the second hump with a crunch of metal and asphalt.

The Ford slowed just enough and Jones stomped the gas. The flathead engine screamed as the car sailed over the second track. Jones hoped the impact would break the Hudson's axle or maybe the driver's head on the steering wheel. After he rounded the next turn, he flipped the dashboard panel down and threw the switches for both taillights and the left headlight, leaving as little for his pursuers to follow as possible. When he looked in the mirror, he saw that the Commodore's headlights were out but the spotlight alongside the driver's window shone like an angry cyclopic eye sweeping the road. A shot whanged off the roof. One bullet in his .45 and three targets, and it didn't look like Jones was going to lose these guys any time soon.

The Hudson was gaining again. The bad guys had one hell of a driver. Ninety-mile-an-hour wind sang through the hole in the windshield like a banshee. The Hudson pulled alongside him, not ramming him this time. They probably figured out he was out of ammo or they wouldn't be so bold. The passenger window was shattered and from the corner of his eye Jones saw the flare of a cigarette lighter. The guy with the snap brim cap was lighting the wick on a bottle. Jones had seen Molotov cocktails in the war, had used them once or twice himself in fact, and he knew what would happen next. His timing had to be just right.

He slammed the brakes, cut the wheel hard left, and double clutched as the thug threw the bottle. Jones saw the startled faces in the glare of his headlight as the car spun. The Ford slewed half off the road barely missing the pine trees along the narrow berm. He wheeled into a classic bootlegger's street turn, the right rear quarter of the Ford slamming the Hudson as it passed. Jones threw the car into gear and as he roared away, he saw the yellow flame blossom in his rear view mirror. He also saw the Hudson clumsily fish-hooking on the narrow two-lane.

An angry whine from the back of the Ford told Jones the impact had bent the fender into the tire. Sooner or later that tire was going to blow, and the boys in the Hudson weren't giving up. Jones weighed his options and watched in his mirror as the Commodore closed on him.

One shot. Jones rolled down his window.

The Hudson pulled alongside him again and didn't bump him. They were going to try another Molotov.

One shot. Jones let go of the steering wheel with one hand and reached for his automatic.

Snap brim lit his lighter.

One shot. Jones thumbed back the hammer of his .45.

Snap Brim lit the rag in the bottle.

One shot. Jones swung the .45 out the window and pulled the trigger.

The bottle shattered in the killer's hand and a ball of fire filled the Hudson. Jones braked hard, and the coupe slid sideways as the Commodore careened ahead, weaving side to side until it went off the road and crashed into the pines. The Ford rolled to a stop and Jones watched the wrecked car. A back door flung open and a flaming man tumbled out. He writhed on the ground for a moment then lay still. The gas tank went up with a whump that hit Jones like a fist in his chest and his face felt a wash of blast furnace heat. Overhead, the pine trees crackled as the flames rose. Jones put the Ford in gear and drove away. Like Hennessey always said, thought Jones, live to fight another day.

CHAPTER THIRTY-FIVE

Two miles down the road Jones saw no lights in either direction. He pulled the car into a grove of trees and popped the trunk. Jones pulled out his shotgun and cocked both hammers then laid it on the bumper while he dug behind the spare tire for the lug wrench. It wasn't the best tool for the job, but in five minutes the Ford's fender was bent away enough to clear the tire as long as it didn't hit any tall bumps or deep chuckholes.

Jones shined a flashlight on the fender and surveyed the damage. Not only was the fender crumpled, but the Hudson's green paint was ground into it. There had been plenty of his paint on the Hudson too, but the fire took care of that. Still, he couldn't drive the Ford around with a bullet hole through the windshield and a smashed fender without attracting attention from the cops and from the son of a bitch who sent the hitters.

He drove back onto the road and headed for the mountains. As the moon came up, he pulled into the hard-packed dirt of Coakee's barnyard. The dogs came out in a pack, barking and snarling. They boiled around the driver's door and Jones hoped none of them came bounding through the jagged glass of the rear windshield.

In a few minutes, Jones saw a light. As it came closer, he realized it was a flashlight taped to the barrel of an over-under shotgun. Jones heard a sharp whistle. The dogs shut up and sat down. It was Coakee.

The light played over the car. "Jones, is that you?"

Jones pushed open the wind wing, not trusting the dogs. "It's me, Coakee."

The light shone on the back fender. "I see why you came. What happened?"

"I had to deliver a 'package' to somebody and somebody else wanted it."

The flashlight snapped off. The voice moved three steps to the side. "Any chance that somebody followed you out here?" Jones realized Coakee shut off the light to prevent making a target of himself.

"Last I saw, there wasn't anybody left to follow."

"Good to hear. Pull it in and let's take a look."

Coakee rolled back the barn door and Jones pulled into the shop. Coakee waited until the door was shut again before turning on the light. "Damn, that fender's a mess."

"I know you can fix it. The question is, how soon. The quicker I'm seen driving an undamaged car around, the quicker people will scratch me off the suspect list."

"I understand. I'd say end of the day tomorrow if I can get the glass cut in Uniontown."

"If you'll give me a lift to the highway, I can hitch back to Brownsville."

"And the 'package'?"

Jones opened the passenger door and pulled out the steel box pocked with bullet holes. "It'll go with me."

Coakee scratched his ear with a grease blackened thumbnail. "Considering what you have there, I don't think hitching's the smartest idea. The cops see you with that case they can't help but be curious." He threw Jones a set of keys. "Take that Buick and bring it back tomorrow to pick up your car." Jones peeled two hundreds from his roll. "Here's some cash to start." He handed it to Coakee, who stuffed the money in the pocket of his overalls without looking at it. "I gotta say, Jones, you make life interesting."

CHAPTER THIRTY-SIX

At three a.m. he parked the Buick three blocks from his hotel and climbed the stairs to his room. In the cracked mirror over the dresser Jones saw the blood and dirt caked on his face. His trousers were ripped at the knees and his jacket had a blood soaked hole where the bullet grazed his shoulder. He thought about washing the blood from his face then thought, time for that later; first things first.

Jones turned the chair to face the door and set the case on the floor beside it. He shut out the light, lit a cigarette, and sat in the chair with the shotgun across his lap. I sensed no magic, Jones thought. These guys were straight up shooters. Who sent them? Malone doesn't seem to be a big enough operator to pay an outfit like that. Was it Benno avenging his son? If so, how did he find me? Who's in this besides Menge? He sat upright in the chair and listened to his own breathing counterpointing the tick of his wristwatch.

Quiet footsteps came soon. Jones saw the shadows of one pair of feet under the door. Someone rapped quietly. He saw light through the keyhole. No one was looking in or trying a key. "Jones, you in there?" Jones knew the voice. It was Danny Hayes.

Jones stood, pointing the shotgun at the center of the door above the shadows of the feet. "Danny, don't move. I have a .12 gauge on the door and you can't jump fast enough to dodge both barrels. The door's not locked. Come in. Slow."

The hinges creaked as the door swung inward. Danny stood silhouetted in the doorway, hands in the classic stickup position. He hesitated for a few seconds then stepped into the room.

"Close the door." Danny did as he was told. "Now, tell me why you're here."

"Skitch sent me. He heard there was trouble tonight and he wanted to know whether you were still…"

"Alive?"

"Yeah, alive."

"And if I have his money, right?"

"Yeah that too."

"You'll understand if I'm a little bit nervous until this gets sorted out. There's nobody else in the hallway, so how about on the stairs or in the street?"

Danny's voice was steady. "Dodie and Sal out back in the car—that's all."

Jones pulled the cord and the light came on. Danny blinked at the light but he looked perfectly calm. No nervous tics or other tells. Jones thought it over for a minute and decided Danny was being straight with him. "Let's go talk to Skitch. You can put your hands down but keep them in sight. Walk two steps ahead of me, no more, no less and remember what I said about the buckshot." Danny nodded, his face impassive and backed into the hallway. Jones looked both ways and seeing no threat, followed him to the stairs, the case in one hand and the shotgun in the other.

"Out the side door and around the block," said Jones. "Come up on the car from behind. No noise." Danny nodded and the pair stepped outside.

Dodie's Mercury was parked down the alley, top down. He and Sal were sitting in the front. Dodie's hands were on the steering wheel. Sal's were in his lap. Jones and Danny came up silently behind the car and Danny whistled softly. Both heads turned to see Jones pointing the shotgun.

"Don't move, Dodie. Guns on the dashboard, boys. Sal, open the door and get out. I'm coming with you, but on my terms." Sal turned toward Dodie and started to speak, but Dodie cut him off with a sharp shake of his head. "Do what he says." Dodie stared first at the case and then at the shotgun. He smiled thinly and said to Jones, "You know that's not necessary."

Jones stared him down as he climbed into the back seat beside Danny. "Tonight people have tried to shoot me, crash my car and burn me alive, and one of them was on our team. At the moment, I don't know exactly who I can trust. But you're right; I don't need the gun." Jones set the shotgun on the floor between his feet and held up a grenade, his fingers wrapped around the safety lever. He smiled broadly to show the pin in his teeth. "Anything funny happens," he said around the pin, "we all say goodnight. Let's go."

Sal stared at the grenade and hesitated for a second then got back in and Dodie started up the Mercury. Nobody said a word as they drove to the poolroom. Bucky let them in the street door, a shotgun under his arm, but he waited below as they climbed the stairs to the elevator, rode to the fourth floor, and crossed the floor of the darkened wire room to Skitch's office. Skitch sat behind his desk, his tie pulled down and his sleeves rolled up. His eyes widened at the sight of the bullet-ridden case and widened further when he saw the grenade. "Jesus Christ Almighty, Jones. What the hell's going on?"

"That's what I'm here to discuss." Jones turned to Dodie, Sal, and Danny and jerked his toward the door. "Outside. Now." The three looked to Skitch and he waved his hand in dismissal. "Go on; it's okay, right, Jones?"

"For the moment."

The trio backed out of the office and closed the door behind them. Jones turned the deadbolt then stepped around to Skitch's side of the desk and set the case on it. "There's your money." He took the pin from his teeth and put it back in the grenade's handle. "What do you know about this?"

Skitch reached in his pocket and saw Jones shift his feet. "Key," said Skitch, "I'm getting the key." He pulled a handful of change from his trouser pocket and dumped it on the desk and rooted through it for the key to the padlock. The lock, undamaged by the gunfire popped open with a sharp click.

Skitch raised the lid and blew out a disgusted breath at the sight of shredded money. "Fifty thousand dollars' worth of confetti. Oh well, I guess it can't all be shot up." He rolled his chair away from the desk and turned it to face Jones. "The boys in New Ken are gonna be pissed off." Skitch turned his hands palms up. "I don't know what went down here anymore than you do, Jones."

"Who knew about the pickup?"

"Dodie and I knew, and Gino at the High Point of course, and you and Vic. That's all."

"And now Gino's driver, and his boy Sonny are dead and so is Vic."

Skitch nodded. "I heard. But you guys got three of their shooters before they got Sonny, Chazz and Vic, right?"

"No, they didn't kill Vic. I did. He was playing for the other side. He signaled them when we got outside then shot Chazz and Sonny. He tried to shoot me too but I got him first. I figure they planned to wing him to make it look good and split the dough later."

"So you took off with the money and they chased you and...?"

"You'll read about them in the obituary column."

Skitch blew out a breath. "So, Jones, you think I set you up? Is that what this is about?" Skitch opened a carved jade box on his desk and took out a cigarette. He put it in his mouth and lit it with his Zippo. "I'd offer you one, but I figure you want both your hands free."

Jones shook his head. "No, I don't think this was your doing. You ran the transfer the right way, covered it with the standard pickup not something special that would call attention to it. You're on the hook for a lot of cash and your reputation's on the line. You have no reason to want me dead unless somebody over your head ordered it, and I don't see that. And it wasn't the Cleveland boys either; one of theirs got hit too.

"The guys who chased me didn't want the money. They were willing to burn up fifty grand to take me out, which means they were being paid a lot more to do the hit. I can think of a few people who'd like to see me dead, but not that much. And you know me well enough now to understand that I'm a tough target. You'd know better than to send a second-stringer like Vic to do the job. Six guys, Skitch, but we probably could have handled them easy if Menge hadn't dusted Sonny and Chazz, and I didn't have to clip Menge."

Skitch shook his head slowly. "I grew up with Vic. I've known him most of my life. I never figured him for a double-crosser."

"Maybe it's not just a double-cross; maybe it's a triple. They dangled some big bucks under Vic's mustache and conned him into believing they were after the cash while I was the real target. Vic kills me, the hitters kill Vic and play it as a heist, and they cover up their real mission. Or maybe if Vic killed me the others would kill Vic and run for it. Whoever wanted to kill me knew enough to send six people to do the job. And then there's the issue of the spot you're in with the Organization. Looks like somebody out there wants me dead and wants to put you out of business in the bargain."

Skitch nodded. "You may be right. The hitters weren't people we knew— the boys from Cleveland either. Gino's men went through their pockets before the cops came. No I.D.s, no labels in the clothing. They were pros – imported talent."

He reached into the case and pulled out a packet of undamaged bills. He counted out twenties and laid them on the desk. "Your money, Vic's money, and an extra C—call it combat pay."

"The cops will be a problem this round," said Jones. Ten guys dead, give or take, a bunch of cars shot up and a hundred or so eyewitnesses."

"That and High Point's in the next county. A blessing and a curse; I'm glad it didn't happen here, but I'll have to trade some pretty big favors out of town to manage this one. So far, nobody fingered you or got your plate number." He reached into a lower desk drawer and handed a license plate to Jones. "Put this on your car and throw the old one in the river, just in case. You might want to stay out of sight for a day or two until we see how this plays out."

"If I hide out, I'll look guilty and I'll look scared. I can't afford either one."

"It's your call, Jones, but it's gonna be tough to hide that cut on your face."

"Do you have a working arrangement with that funeral home up the hill?"

"Cerullo's? Yeah, you could say we cooperate with each other."

"Wake him up. Tell him I'm coming and to warm up the wax."

"Okay, I'll call him right away." After a quick turn on the phone Skitch turned to Jones and said, "Be at the back door in an hour."

"I guess that's it then. You open the door, Skitch. I don't want any more surprises tonight." Skitch got up and pulled back the deadbolt. He opened the door and over his shoulder Jones could see Dodie, Sal and Danny, guns aimed at the doorway. Skitch put his hands palms up. "It's copacetic. Put 'em away." The men hesitated a few seconds, then Dodie lowered his pistol and the others followed suit.

Skitch said to Dodie and the others. "No hard feelings, boys. It's just business, right?" No reply. He turned to Jones. "You want a ride back to your place?

Jones shook his head. "I'll walk." Danny and Sal took him down in the elevator while Dodie waited behind to talk with Skitch. On the street, Jones leaned into the back seat of Dodie's Merc and retrieved his shotgun. Instead of going back to his room, Jones climbed the hill toward the castle and the cemetery. With time to kill he sat in a far corner of the graveyard with his back against a thick granite tombstone his feet aimed toward another, the shotgun across his thighs.

He lit a cigarette, cupping his hand around the flare. Only one on the match this time. That's twice now, Jones thought. The coal dock didn't work so they had to try harder. Somebody willing to throw away fifty grand to kill me must think I'm one hell of a threat. It's time to prove them right.

CHAPTER THIRTY-SEVEN

Jones was still awake when Marty shoved the paper under his door. He turned it over. No headline about the High Point incident; it happened too late for the paper to cover it, but it would be half a page tomorrow. Plenty of time to get his car back and be seen around town looking innocent.

He'd sat up in the chair all night rather than risk sleeping in the bed and undoing the job Carlo Cerullo had done on his face. The cut wasn't really bad enough to demand stitches, but Carlo cleaned away the caked blood and sutured it anyway to keep it from reopening and dislodging the thin layer of mortician's wax he applied to Jones's cheek. A little light make up, and from further than three feet, Jones's face looked as if nothing had ever happened to it.

Jones looked in the mirror. Comb his hair and put on a clean shirt, and no one would guess he was in a gun battle the night before. He slid his .45 into its shoulder rig, put on his jacket, and went to breakfast. It will be interesting, he thought, to see who looks surprised.

As he crossed under the bridge to Fiddle's, Jones saw two town cops leaving the diner. When he first came to Brownsville, the cops gave him a once over every time one of them saw him. Now that they associated him with Skitch, their eyes seemed to look past him as if he wasn't there. Today was no exception.

Jones sat at a booth in the back facing the door. Ellie brought him coffee and a smile that faded into a look of curiosity. "You in a fist fight?"

Jones gave her a one-sided smile. "No, not me. Why would you say that?"

"Your face looks a little puffy, that's all."

"Got a bad tooth. It hurts like hell."

"Better go see a dentist." Ellie looked unconvinced but didn't press it. "So you want your usual?"

"Yeah, and bring me a glass of orange juice too, and a couple of aspirins if you have them."

She jotted the order on her pad. "I'll bring it right out," she said over her shoulder heading for the kitchen.

Jones sipped his coffee and breathed the steam from the cup into his nostrils. Live to fight another day, he thought, certain that the fight was far from over.

When Ellie came back to refill his cup, Jones said, "Got any plans for tonight?"

She wiped a strand of hair from her forehead. "I work 'til five."

"After that?"

"Nothing special," she said. "What did you have in mind?"

"I saw that big hotel up on the mountain past Uniontown a couple of weeks ago. Sign said dining and dancing nightly. I thought maybe you'd like to eat a steak instead of serving one for a change."

Ellie put a hand on her hip. "Jones, are you asking me out?"

Jones nodded. "I guess so. After dinner maybe you can teach me to dance."

Ellie thought about it for a minute then smiled. "Okay, Jones, you've got yourself a date. Pick me up at seven. If I start now, it'll take me until then to decide what to wear, my green dress or my blue one."

"I've got it easy. I only have one suit. No need to choose."

"Seven then," said Ellie, and she scurried off to retrieve an order from the kitchen.

CHAPTER THIRTY-EIGHT

Jones had some time to kill before he started over the mountain to pick up his car so he opted to walk across town, cross the creek, and look for Granny Maybelle. A few blocks from Snowdon Square a rickety bridge

"…no one would guess he was in a gun battle…"

crossed the Redstone Creek. Jones read once that George Washington had fished in it in years past and called it one of the best trout streams in Pennsylvania. Now it ran a sickly orange from mine drainage. "Yellowboy," said Jones aloud. Iron hydroxide from mining waste mixed with sulfur from the coal killed anything animate in the water. The price of prosperity.

The path wound for more than a mile through the trees along the stinking creek to a cluster of buildings more akin to shacks than houses. Grey unpainted wood cobbled together with rusted nails. Dirty barefoot children, black and white played in the trampled earth that comprised yards. From a frayed rope, two of them hung on an old truck tire and swung back and forth. The children froze at the sight of a stranger and as if on command all backed away from Jones. As they backed away, men and women in clean but threadbare clothing came out of the shacks, like a parody of a Swiss clock. They stood still and stared at him silently with eyes as dead as marbles then began slowly closing in.

Jones felt the tug of magic then a voice spoke behind him. "Mister Jones." The villagers stopped advancing. Jones turned to see Granny Maybelle's messenger, the boy with different colored eyes. "You come to see Granny Maybelle," a statement not a question. "She been waiting for you. This way." The men and women stepped back and allowed Jones to follow the boy past their makeshift village and deeper into the woods.

Granny Maybelle lived in a brick bungalow that seemed oddly out of place in the middle of the trees and mountain laurel. It was as if the house had been plucked from some *Saturday Evening Post* cover and dropped from the sky. The cultivated patch to its side teemed with herbs, flowers, and roots found in no ordinary garden. Jones recognized foxglove, belladonna, and a host of others used for healing and for spells.

Jones's tattoos began to twitch and as the door to the bungalow swung open, they began to throb. The wards were powerful. This was the nexus of the magic he'd encountered since he came to Brownsville, or was it? The magic he felt here, if it had a color, would be green, in league with the Earth and all that grew on it. What he felt before was blackness.

Granny Maybelle stepped from the shadows of the house into the dappled light of the clearing. She was elderly, but not stooped with age as so many older people become. Her carriage was erect, almost regal as she crossed the yard to him. She wore a faded calico dress that sagged on her once fuller figure, a white shawl draped over her shoulders. Granny Maybelle's face was angular though it had once been round. Cancer, thought Jones.

Her hair was white and he guessed that undone, the single braid she wore would have hung almost to her feet. It wound instead three times around her head, crisscrossing and making a sort of diadem at her forehead. Beneath it, her golden irises almost glowed around ebony pupils.

"Mister Jones," despite her age, her voice was fluid, almost hypnotic in its timbre. "I have been waiting for you. Please come in."

Jones wiped his feet on the rough straw mat at the doorsill and stepped inside. He had to duck passing through the low door frame to prevent knocking off his hat, which he took off out of respect to the elderly woman.

"Welcome to my home, Mister Jones. Please, sit," she said, gesturing to an old but immaculately clean sofa, the nap of the chenille worn shiny under crocheted antimacassars.

Jones looked around the room. The walls were covered with framed photographs, many of them portraits of black men and women, individuals and families while others showed landscapes worthy of Ansel Adams but not of pristine peaks and river valleys. These showed the spidery structures of coal tipples towering over blackened ground, the smoking mounds of slag heaps, and the devil's breath of endless ranks of beehive coke ovens. Many of the faces captured by camera's eye were so blackened with coal dust as to make race indistinguishable. All were one under the ground. The artistry the photographs represented was unmistakable.

"My husband Bertram, may he rest in peace, was a photographer—not for a living, mind you—he worked as a mason and a bricklayer for the mines. Bertram built this house with his hands, but taking pictures was his avocation."

"They are remarkable work," said Jones. "These belong in a gallery. I've never seen any better."

"I thank you," Granny said. "I believe what he did with his camera was its own sort of magic. I have just made some tea. Would you like some?"

"Thank you, yes. That would be very welcome."

Jones sat on the sofa as Granny disappeared into the kitchen. She returned in a moment with a tray. She poured a steaming cup for Jones and he inhaled its bouquet but waited to take his first sip. The aroma was rich with herbs and spices. "The boy..."

"Ephriam."

"Yes. Ephriam said the 'bad thing' was here and worse was coming. Please tell me what that means."

"I think you know already, Mister Jones." She poured herself a cup of the steaming brew. "You have been here how long?"

"About two months. Am I the 'bad thing'?"

"There is bad, and there is worse." Her words radiated authority and control. She lifted her cup and drank a swallow. "Please enjoy your tea, Mister Jones. I assure you it is quite safe."

"I…"

Granny Maybelle held up a hand. "I understand your caution. You are a man whose life depends upon it. But you need have no fear of me. We are, if not exactly on the same side of things, dealing with a common foe. Magic forges odd alliances, does it not?"

Jones stared at her over the rim of his cup as he drank his tea. "The 'worse' thing is coming? I've seen magic at work here, but I don't know its source."

Granny Maybelle smiled. "Nor do I, but you will find it and root it out if you can, because that is your nature. When you arrived, I sensed your presence, but I felt no menace in you. You are gifted, but up to now you have used that gift to pursue violent ends. What magic you use has been given to you, against your will, perhaps, but you have learned to use it of necessity, and I do not judge you for it."

"And your magic?"

"I use what I have been taught to heal and to aid those in distress who have nowhere else to turn."

"Like the people back there in that shanty town?"

"Yes." She set down her cup and filled it again. "They are all my children in a sense. Had Ephriam not called you away, they would have given their lives to keep you away from me. I have no doubt that you would have killed many of them, but I believe their numbers would have prevailed."

Jones thought of the dead eyed rabble and realized the truth of Granny Maybelle's words. "But, I am here for good or for ill."

"Yes. I would hope for good."

"You want me to fight this battle for you. Just like the Army, just like the mob."

"No, Mister Jones, not for me; I wish you to fight this battle for the greater good in ways that I cannot."

"I have fought evil, if you want to call it that, in the past, but as you said, there is bad and there is worse. 'Good' is often defined by the greater might."

"You are far wiser than I hoped you would be, Mister Jones." She reached into a pocket of her dress and drew out a leather drawstring pouch the size of her hand. "I will do my part. I offer you this charm as protection so long as you labor against evil, but I warn you that if you turn to badness, the charm will work against you with the same force."

Jones took the pouch and ran his thumb over it, feeling the odd shapes inside. His tattoos hummed but not with discomfort. He reached to untie the thick knot in the drawstring, and Granny Maybelle said sharply, "No, Mister Jones! Do not open the pouch lest you release the power inside it. Like Pandora's Box, once done, it can never be undone."

Jones stared at the pouch for a moment and slipped it into the pocket of his jacket. "I understand. Thank you."

"Ephriam will guide you back to your path. Once you have left this place, you will be hard put to find it again on your own. Be very careful, Mister Jones." She rose and opened the door. "I wish you well."

In a few moments, Jones was following Ephriam along the sulfurous creek. He looked over his shoulder and saw that the path behind him had become a thick tangle of green. Overhead the skies had darkened. A storm is coming, thought Jones, and it will be a big one.

CHAPTER THIRTY-NINE

Jones was right. By the time he rolled Coakee's Buick onto Route 40, sheets of rain turned the streets a uniform shade of gunmetal grey. As he pulled into the barnyard, lightning blazed and rain poured from the black clouds. The dogs, content to stay under the shelter of a lean-to barked furiously and in a minute, Coakee rolled the door open and motioned for Jones to pull the car inside.

In a corner near the door, one of Coakee's men was finishing the seal on the rear windshield of the Ford. Another was polishing the restored fender with a rag. "We lucked out and found a fender from the same model and the same color at a junkyard down the road. I put a used tire on the back as close to the others as I could find. Never know you were in a scrape to look at the car, Jones," said Coakee with a chuckle. He looked Jones up and down. "Nor your face, neither."

"It's always helpful to know talented people, Coakee." Jones peeled several bills off his roll. "Take out what I owe you." Coakee plucked a few bills from the wad and handed the rest back to Jones.

Jones handed Coakee the new license plate and Coakee took a screwdriver from the wall rack. "I took a look at the underside too," said

Coakee, undoing the screws on the new license plate. "Nothing broken, but I'd get the wheels aligned soon as you can."

In five minutes, Jones was on his way back to Brownsville.

He parked the coupe on the street below the poolroom and went inside. Let everyone see the car without a scratch, and him too. As he started up the stairs, he saw Dodie at the back table shooting nine ball with Sal. They eyed him coldly. Neither was forgiving nor forgetting.

A hot shower in the locker room made Jones feel human again. As he started down the stairs, he met Skitch coming up. "Where you headed?"

"To get a haircut."

"Oh yeah? Come on to the basement with me."

Jones had never been in the cellar before. When Skitch pulled the chain and the light came on, he was surprised to see a barber chair, gleaming with polished brass and red leather. "Have a seat," Skitch said, snapping a white chair cape.

"You cut hair too?"

"I was a barber for years before I moved up in the Organization," he said. "I used to cut Salvatore Dragone's hair every Friday along with his whole crew. A lot of business was done down here. I kept my ears open and my mouth shut, and before too long, I was part of the operation."

Jones sat in the chair and Skitch chose a long metal comb and a pair of barber shears from the shelf behind him. "Carlo does nice work. I can't even see the cut and I know it's there."

"Yeah, but it won't last forever. I had to be really careful washing up, and I'll have to watch it shaving too."

"I can help you there," said Skitch, "if you trust me put a razor under your chin." He laughed.

"You wouldn't cut my throat, Skitch. I'm too useful, this week at least."

Done trimming his hair, Skitch worked up a lather in the shaving mug. Jones said, "There's no ill will from Danny; we understand each other, but Dodie and Sal are still burning over last night. Anybody else?"

"The New Ken crew isn't happy, and neither are the Cleveland boys, but more of the money was intact than wasn't. Nobody's blaming you, Jones. You did your part and you delivered the goods. When they find out who queered this deal, they'll be fast and nasty. As for Dodie and Sal, they'll get over it. They just aren't used to being trumped."

"What about the cops?"

"It's being managed by people way over my head. Raise your chin a little."

Ten minutes later, Jones walked out of the poolroom looking better than he had in a long time.

CHAPTER FORTY

Mickey Malone was never comfortable around his new boss. The man wore a silk hood that covered his head except for two eyeholes. Malone understood he'd want to hide his identity, but it gave him the creeps just the same. And when Malone asked him, "What do I call you?" all he said was, "'Sir' will do." Malone was always good at picking winners, however, and was convinced he was on the right team this time. He pulled into the rutted lane that led a couple of hundred yards through a dense stand of pines to an old stone house.

He knocked three quick and two slow and turned the knob. The door was never locked, another item that made Malone nervous. Anybody who had no fear alone out here was either crazy or dangerous as hell. Malone was convinced that Sir was anything but crazy.

The voice came from upstairs. "Come."

From the basement, Malone heard snuffling and grunting. As he climbed the creaking staircase, his fingers were clammy on the banister. He had nothing to fear; he was on the winning team, so why was he afraid? Malone followed the hallway to the back of the house and opened the door to a darkened room.

His boss sat in a tall wing chair, elbows on the arms and fingers steepled in front of his chest. Red today, thought Malone, regarding the silk hood. Malone stood in the center of the room, hands clutching the brim of his hat like a schoolboy in the principal's office.

"I understand that our efforts have failed," said the harsh voice.

"Yes, Sir. Jones got away, money and all. He killed all six of our men."

"Oh, that troublesome Mr. Jones," said Sir. "I have another plan that will perhaps meet our needs in many ways at once."

As Sir detailed his orders, Malone felt a cold bead of sweat trickle down his spine as he realized that he was in way over his head and there was nothing he could do about it.

CHAPTER FORTY-ONE

At exactly seven o'clock Jones pulled up to Ellie's boarding house. He liked Ellie a lot, but that wasn't the only reason for the evening out. Jones figured that he should be away from his room and Snowdon Square tonight, and that the people who wanted to hit him would be less likely to try it in a public place. The rain that had pounded Brownsville all afternoon had finally stopped but the water dripped from the elms in front of the house and spotted Jones's suit and hat. He raised his hand but the door swung inward before he could knock. A short woman with a round face and her hair in a grey bun said, "Yes?"

Jones took off his hat and said politely, "C. O. Jones. I'm here to see Ellie, ma'am."

She looked him over and stepped back to let him inside then smiled. "She'll be down in a minute. Come into the parlor and sit down."

In the next five minutes, Jones learned enough about Mrs. Surovchak, her family and her neighbors to fill five dossiers. About the time she got around to questioning Jones about his pedigree, Ellie appeared in the doorway. Jones had to admit her outfit took her a long way from the diner. Ellie wore a green dress cinched tight at her narrow waist. The top buttoned in a diagonal placket that ran from her belt to peaked shoulders and short sleeves. The skirt hugged her hips just right and ended just below her knees. Her hair was swept up and around her head and secured with a tortoise shell comb.

Jones stood. "Wow, you look great, Ellie."

She gave him a mock frown. "Don't act so surprised, Jones. And now that I think about it, you don't look too shabby either." She turned to the landlady. "I'm not sure what time I'll be back, Mrs. Surovchak, so I'll take my key. No need for you to wait up." Ellie offered her arm to Jones, and they walked out the front door into the evening.

Before they were out of Brownsville, Ellie had the radio on and was turning the dial looking for music. She settled on Guy Lombardo and the Royal Canadians playing "Imagination."

Neither spoke much for a while, just listening to the music and the hum of the Ford's engine. Finally Ellie broke the silence. "So, Jones, do you miss the coal dock?"

He shrugged. "It was just one more job. I've had better and I've had worse."

"I guess it's better now," she said, "if you can afford to take me to the Summit for dinner."

Jones smiled, never taking his eyes off the road. "No argument there."

Ellie watched him for a moment. "Is somebody following us?"

"Why would you say that?"

"You haven't looked at me since you started the engine. Your eyes keep shifting from the road to the mirror."

"I'm just a careful driver. Never hurts to be safe." He turned his head toward her and winked. "I promise I'll get you there in one piece."

She turned her head toward the window. "It's not me I worry about, Jones," she said quietly. "Not one bit."

The Summit Hotel looked like an oversized Victorian mansion, gleaming white, fresh washed by the rain as Jones pulled into the drive and under the portico. A uniformed bellhop stepped up as Jones rolled down his window. "Dinner or overnight guest, sir?"

"Dinner," said Jones.

"Parking for dinner guests is to the right, sir. Would the lady like to get out here?"

Jones looked to Ellie. She nodded and the bellhop ran around the car to open her door. She stepped out of the car smoothing her dress. "I'll wait on the porch."

Jones found a space in the crowded lot and backed into it. He climbed the broad staircase and found Ellie at the far end of the porch gazing at a spectacular view of the valley. The late day sun painted a tinge of gold to everything below. "Even if you didn't buy me dinner, Jones, this view would be worth the ride. It's beautiful."

"Best part of it all, you get both." He took her arm and led her through a regal lobby, all polished oak and thick carpeting, to the dining room. "It's crowded," said Ellie. "Do you think we'll have to wait long for a table?"

"Probably not." Jones stepped up to the podium and said, "Jones, reservation for two."

The tuxedoed maitre d' said, "Yes, sir, this way please."

The dining room was as elegant as the lobby, linens and silver immaculate and fine china place settings. Jones held out Ellie's chair. "You're right. I've been working in the diner too long. I'd forgotten what dining out could be like."

Jones ordered steaks for them both and a bottle of red wine. "A habit I brought back from Europe," he said. "Everyone has wine with dinner."

"Why's that?"

"I guess it's safer than drinking the water."

By the time they had finished eating, music drifted from the downstairs bar. A quartet: piano, drums, upright bass, and trumpet were playing "Moonglow." The bar was as busy as the dining room, but they found an empty table at the back of the room. "Now, Jones, it's time to dance."

Dancing wasn't as difficult as Jones thought it might be. Ellie was proficient and confident, and she guided Jones through the first fumbling song or two until he caught the rhythm of it. Soon he was leading her and managed to navigate the crowded dance floor without stepping on her toes too many times. When the band started "In the Mood," Ellie pulled him off the floor to their table. "I don't think we're quite ready to jitterbug," she said with a laugh.

The waitress brought a whiskey and soda for Jones and when Ellie ordered a Manhattan his eyebrows rose. "Don't look so surprised, Jones," she said. "I said I grew up on a farm, not that I lived on one my whole life."

Jones looked around the room as he sipped his drink, pleased at the contrast between the Summit and the High Point and its boilermaker crowd. After midnight the people began drifting out in twos and groups, and as the band played its last few numbers, Jones heard the rumble of thunder. "Guess we'd better get going," he said. Ellie agreed and they climbed the stairs to the lobby. Outside the rain hammered the parking lot and lightning blazed across the sky.

"Looks like a bad drive down the mountain," said Ellie.

"Probably so," said Jones. "Well, we could wait it out or I could always get us two rooms and we could stay the night." Ellie shrugged and Jones said, "I'll check at the desk." In ten minutes, a bellhop led them up the broad oak staircase to the second floor and a pair of adjoining rooms. He opened the first and Ellie stepped inside. Then he opened the second. Jones tipped him and went back to Ellie's room where she waited in the open doorway.

"Good thing tomorrow's Sunday and I don't have to work," she said. "It's been a nice evening, Jones. Goodnight." She rose on tiptoe to kiss him and stepped back into her room and closed the door. Jones went into his room and closed his door too. He hung his jacket in the armoire and hung his necktie over the back of a chair. The pistol went on the nightstand.

He was sitting on the bed untying his shoes when he heard the bolt slide on the connecting door. In a second Ellie tapped on it lightly. He opened the bolt from his side and she opened the door from hers. She was still dressed but her hair was down in dark waves across her shoulders. "I guess I was a little brusque with you," she said. "I'm sorry for that, but I'm just not used to this yet."

Jones put his hands on the doorframe. "No apology necessary. You know what's best for you. It was a good time for me tonight too. She leaned in and kissed him again and this time gave him a chance to kiss her back. "Maybe you should sleep on it," he said. "We can talk about it in the morning."

"You're one of the good guys, Jones," Ellie said and after a pause, gently closed the door. Jones heard the bolt slide into place and wondered if she really meant it. Better to keep things in separate compartments, he thought. He liked Ellie a lot but romance didn't seem like a good idea at the moment. Then again, in his life when did it ever?

CHAPTER FORTY-TWO

Jones was asleep for about an hour when he heard the bolt slide on the connecting door. His hand slid across the bed to the nightstand as the door slowly opened. He saw Ellie silhouetted in the doorway by a dim light from her room. When she turned, he could see she was nude. "Jones," she whispered. He didn't answer at first, waiting and watching. "Jones, are you awake?"

"Yeah, I'm awake."

"I decided I don't need to sleep on it."

She turned back the sheet in the darkness and climbed into the bed beside him. Ellie took his face in her hands and kissed him hard. Her hand slid down from his face to his throat and across his chest then stopped. She slid her hand a little further and stopped again, her breath catching in a gasp. "Oh, my God!"

"Olly olly oxen free," Jones said. He turned on the bedside lamp and Ellie gazed openmouthed at his chest. The glossy puckered scars shone in the soft glow and the tattoos stood out like stark shadows. "I had no idea," she said. Then her eye caught the fresh wound in Jones's shoulder. "That's new," she said. "When did that happen?"

"Last night."

Ellie dragged her nails over his cheek dislodging the mortician's wax and exposing the sutures on his cheek. "I knew it! Damn, you, Jones!" she said, anger swelling in her voice. "You make me care for you and all the time you're leaning over an open grave. How could you do this to…"

Jones stopped her tirade by kissing her. She struggled at first but finally gave in to passion and in a moment, they were well past talking.

Later as they lay in a tangle of bedclothes, Ellie said, "When did you plan to tell me?"

"I didn't plan. I never figured it would get this far. It just did."

"Okay, the scars I understand. You fought in a war, but the tattoos I don't understand. Other guys have hearts with their girlfriends' names and pin up girls and . . . I don't know . . . American flags. But these?"

Jones lit a cigarette and blew a cloud of smoke at the ceiling. "Some guys got gas masks. I got wards."

"Wards?"

"Protective symbols."

"To protect you from what?"

And for the next hour the story poured out of Jones, the Sight, Madame Lavois, Hennessey, the good guys and the bad guys and the real horrors of war. When he was through, he lay beside Ellie and for the first time he could remember, felt relief from his unique burden.

She was quiet for a long time and finally said, "I never had any idea..."

"Most people don't. If the average Joe knew just what our government and all the others were up to, he'd put a gun in his mouth."

"But why are you working for Skitch Mottolla's crew?"

"I got out of the Army with no real skills for a regular job, so I do what I know best. All we can do is move on day to day. What else is there?"

"But that's just survival."

Jones turned to look into her eyes. "Maybe there's more to it. Time will tell."

Ellie put her arm across Jones's chest and pressed against him. She laid her head on his shoulder and didn't move until morning. Maybe she slept.

CHAPTER FORTY-THREE

Jerry turned the car into Pearl Street and pulled up in front of Skitch's house. He stepped around to open Skitch's door, hand in his coat and eyes out for trouble. Skitch stepped onto the sidewalk. "Thanks, Jerry. I won't need you in the morning. I'll drive the family to church."

"Yes, sir."

The house was one step short of a mansion, two and a half stories of red brick with a wraparound porch and a *porte cochere*. Not bad, thought

Skitch, for a poor Ginzo kid from the West Side. The porch light was off but a lamp glowed through the living room curtains, Tillie's signal that she was waiting up for him. Skitch turned the key and stepped inside.

Tillie was waiting for him in her old chenille bathrobe, hair in rollers, but she still looked like a movie star. Soft music played on a radio around the corner. "About time you came home," she snorted.

"It's never too late to come home, babe." The exchange was the kind of old joke that comes from comfort and familiarity as much as love.

"Hungry?" she said. Skitch nodded. "Come on in the kitchen. I'll heat you up some food."

Skitch sat down to veal, potatoes and green beans. As he ate, Tillie rattled on about the relatives, the neighbors, and Frankie. "Frankie said a word today." She cocked an eyebrow at him.

"What word?"

"*The* word. If he's gonna pick up that kind of language from your goombahs…"

A crash sounded from the living room. Skitch jumped from his chair. "Stay here." He ran into the dining room, opened the door of the liquor cabinet, and pulled out a pistol. He turned the corner and froze at what he saw.

The front door was splintered out of its frame and standing in the doorway was a man, or something that looked like a man. The intruder was naked, and Skitch could see every swollen muscle and tendon in his body straining to break through his skin. His chest bulged like a hogshead and his head seemed to meld into brutal shoulders with no neck between. Dark red eyes loured from deep sunken sockets in a parody of a human face.

Massive arms raised at the beast's side and the hands twisted into cruel claws. It lumbered across the room and Skitch fired three shots, a fourth into its chest without effect. The man-thing grunted and twisted its torso, backhanding Skitch and knocking him to the floor. The pistol went skidding across the carpet. Tillie was screaming. Skitch scrambled to his feet and grabbed a chair by the legs. He swung it hard, breaking it over the creature's head.

The man-thing turned and grabbed Skitch by the shoulders. It lifted him from the floor like a doll and threw him across the room to crash into the wall. It stepped toward him and clumsily raised a foot to crush his skull. From upstairs Skitch heard Frankie's voice. "Mama? Mama?" The creature paused, tilted its head upward and stepped over Skitch. As Skitch lost consciousness, the last thing he heard was Tillie's screaming, and the last sight he saw was the creature ponderously, deliberately climbing the stairs to the second floor.

CHAPTER FORTY-FOUR

When Jones dropped Ellie off in the morning he walked her to the door. She rose on tiptoe and kissed him lightly on the mouth.

"Aren't you worried that Mrs. Surovchak will be scandalized?"

She smiled. "Since I didn't come home last night, I'm sure she's figured it out."

Jones climbed the stairs to his room wrestling with the thought that now he had another reason to . . . how did Granny Maybelle put it . . . root out the evil. He stopped at the head of the stairs. His door was ajar.

Jones pulled his automatic and flattened against the wall, inching quietly down the hallway to the doorway. He took a breath and kicked the door. It swung inward and banged against the wall. His gun hand whipped from side to side. No one was there. Across the room, a small paper sack stood on the dresser.

He closed the door behind him and locked it so that no one could sneak in behind him. He carefully pulled back the top edge of the sack and looked inside to see the top of a tall, skinny olive jar. Jones pushed the sack down, exposing the jar and stared in disbelief.

"No. No!" he said.

Looking back at him from the jar were two bloody eyeballs, one brown and one green.

Footsteps in the hall. One pair of feet. Pounding on the door. "Jones! Jones! Open up!" He recognized Danny Hayes's voice. He pulled the bag back over the bottle and threw it in the top drawer of the dresser.

Jones opened the door and Danny Hayes stumbled in. He was wild-eyed and desperate. Words tumbled out of his mouth in a jumble. "Where have you been? I've been trying to find you. You have to come—it's—I don't know what—Skitch…" Jones grabbed Danny and shook him by his shoulders. "What? What happened?"

"The boy. The boy."

"What boy, Ephriam?"

"No, Skitch's boy Frankie. It took him."

"It? What it? What are you talking about?"

"...Skitch fired three shots..."

"A thing. It came into Skitch's house and took the boy."

"What kind of thing?"

"It was like a man, but it was big, and its arms and chest, like boulders…"

"Where's Skitch now?"

"He's at his house with Tillie. She was hysterical. The doc gave her a shot to quiet her down."

"Let's go." As they drove across town to Skitch's house, Jones saw people in suits and dresses going into one church or another, oblivious to the terror that had arrived in Brownsville and feeling secure in their hope that crosses, stained glass and incense would deliver them from evil.

Jones felt a chill. Granny Maybelle was right. The worse thing had arrived, or was something still worse on the way?

Jones pulled up behind a line of cars he recognized from Snowdon Square plus two cop cars. Sal and Jerry stood shoulder to shoulder with two harness bulls on the porch at either side of the splintered front door, guns in their hands. He and Danny went inside and found Dodie and Skitch sitting on the sofa. A pair of coffee cups sat on the coffee table beside a sawed off shotgun, a bottle of whiskey and two shot glasses. Skitch sat with his head in his hands, elbows on his knees. He looked up when Jones came in, and Jones saw the red rims of sleeplessness around his eyes, that and a baseball sized bruise on the side of his face.

"Christ, Jones, you've got to help me."

"Tell me what happened, Skitch."

He shook his head slowly. "It was late, around eleven thirty. I came home and Tillie fixed me some food. We were in the kitchen when I heard a crash. I ran into the living room, and that's when I saw it."

"What did you see?"

"It was a man, or looked like a man, but he was all puffed up, like in the Popeye cartoons when he blows in his thumb and his arms pop out, but all of him; every goddamned muscle. I keep a gun in the liquor cabinet over there, and I got it out and didn't wait to ask questions. I shot him four times and he just kept coming. He knocked the gun out of my hand and threw me into the wall. I went down, and he just stepped over me like I didn't matter and walked up the stairs.

"The light wasn't good, Jones, but I swear his face looked like Tony Motsko's."

CHAPTER FORTY-FIVE

The big question on everyone's mind was what the kidnapper wanted. If it was money, Skitch was ready to pay any amount to have Frankie back. Jones feared the boy was taken for other reasons, ones he'd rather not think about. When the call came soon after dark, Jones and Dodie were with Skitch in his office. Jones answered the phone on the second ring. "Hello."

There was silence at the other end then, "You're not Mottolla. Put him on." There was something odd about the voice that Jones couldn't quite place.

Skitch held the phone so that Jones could hear the conversation. "This is Skitch Mottolla."

"I have something that belongs to you. I believe you have something that belongs to me."

"What's that?"

"A statue approximately eight inches tall, a figure of a horned man cast in pewter."

It's not pewter, thought Jones. Skitch looked up at the statue sitting on the shelf behind his desk. "I won that statue in a card game from Mike Donvan…"

"Who stole it from me in a half-witted burglary."

"Well for God's sake, why didn't you just ask me for it?"

"It's not your place to question me. The statue for the boy; do we deal?"

"This isn't how we do things, pal. We leave family out of it."

"Perhaps this is not how you do things, but it is how I do them . . . pal." The precise delivery and the emphasis on the last word radiated contempt and sneering superiority.

Skitch looked at Jones who scribbled a note and held it up for Skitch to see: ask to talk to Frankie. "I need to know the boy is alive and will be when you get what you want."

"Very well." There was some shuffling at the other end of the line. "Call to your father, Frankie."

"Daddy!" Jones could tell by Skitch's frantic expression that it was Frankie's voice. Then an ungodly scream blared from the earpiece.

Skitch turned pale. "Frankie!"

The voice was back. "As you see, pal, he's alive for the moment. How long he lives depends on your cooperation. Here's how it's going to go. I will call you shortly to give you directions. When I have the statue, you may have the boy. No police. One other detail: I want your man Jones to deliver it, alone."

Skitch and Jones looked at each other. Jones nodded.

"Okay," said Skitch. "I'll have Jones bring it to you. But my men'll have to find him."

"Don't toy with me, Mottolla. He answered your phone. Remember: alone."

"Okay, alone."

"If I have any indication that others are involved, you will bury your son in a very small box. Understood?"

"Yeah. Understood. But you better…" The line went dead.

Skitch was quiet for a long time before he spoke. "Why does he want you, Jones, and how does he know you?"

"I'm not sure." But he does want me, thought Jones, and that's what this is really all about.

"Do we trust him?"

"No, but we take him seriously." Jones lifted the statue from the shelf and looked into its decadent, smirking face. He said to Dodie, "Get Danny Hayes up here. We have to move fast. We need men and cars right now. We might have fifteen minutes, we might have an hour. We'll do what we can. Who do you know in town who loads ammo?"

"We have loading equipment in the basement," said Dodie. "We do our own."

Jones said, "Good. Bring me a saw, a drill and a file as quick as you can."

The call came nearly an hour later. Skitch answered.

"Put Jones on the line." Skitch handed Jones the phone.

"This is Jones."

"Mister Jones, bring the statue to the old Magnus warehouse at the end of Kyle road. You have thirty minutes or the deal is off. No tricks. I think you know what you're dealing with." The line clicked and the phone went dead. Something clicked in Jones's head as well and he suddenly understood what it was all about.

"Okay," said Jones. "How do I get to the Magnus warehouse?"

CHAPTER FORTY-SIX

The Magnus Company warehouse was an ugly brick pile that sat on the opposite bank of the Monongahela River. Jones and Danny studied it through binoculars in the pale light of a full moon. It lay on a knob of land that projected into the river and had only one road in or out. One side of the building hung slightly over the bank above the water, and a small pier stood below.

Jones said. "What do you think, Danny?"

Danny swept the binoculars over the scene again. "I figure they'll come and go by a boat on the river, otherwise they'd be too vulnerable trying to get away."

"That's how I'd play it."

Jones opened the trunk of his coupe. He pulled out the Mauser sniper rifle. "How good are you with one of these?"

Danny looked through the scope. "Better than average. No wind tonight, but it's more than three hundred yards in the dark, the moon aside."

"How about from a spot on the same side of the river?"

Danny picked up the binoculars again. "That switching tower up the tracks to the right would give me a clear shot all the way down river once they clear the dock. If they go upriver, it'll be chancy."

"That's the best we've got."

"What if they cut straight across the river?"

"Skitch will have men blocking the road both ways on this side."

"I gotta say, Jones, I don't like this much."

And you'd like it even less if you knew exactly what you were fighting, he thought. "Me either, Danny, but we play the hand that's dealt us." Jones pulled the statue from the pocket of his jacket. "I have one choice: show up with this."

Jones knew that there was no alternative to bringing the statue. Anyone who used magic would recognize a fake as soon as he set foot in the warehouse. But maybe he wouldn't notice if a little bit were missing. So, Jones had quickly sawn off a half inch from the base of the statue and he divided it into two pieces. The larger piece Dodie cast into slugs and loaded into bullets. The smaller piece Jones drilled and ground into a crude ring that fit his little finger. From the moment Jones slipped it on, he felt his tattoos humming. He hoped it would enhance the Sight. If ever he needed an edge, this was the time.

CHAPTER FORTY-SEVEN

Jones turned the Ford around and parked it aiming back the way he had come. The access road to the warehouse was paved but it was narrow and in bad repair. No easy getaways. He got out of the car looking in every direction. The parking lot was empty. The windows of the warehouse were black holes in the face of the deserted building. The only sounds were the lapping of the river and the calls of crickets and frogs.

Jones walked straight to the open door of the warehouse. If someone were going to shoot him it would have happened already. He wants me, thought Jones, and he wants me for something other than a quick easy death.

Moonlight shone through the broken widows and Jones saw that the warehouse was littered with the bones of a defunct business; discarded mining machinery, wheels, gears, steel shafts, and old office furniture; a filing cabinet with a missing drawer, a desk bent down in the center, a broken chair. Jones stood still in the middle of the open space. The statue-metal ring sharpened his senses preternaturally. No sound, no tingle of strange magic. He was alone for the moment.

In the distance, Jones heard the sound of a motor. It was a speedboat coming from upriver. He'd been right. In a moment, the motor died and Jones heard footsteps, four or five people coming up the stairs from the lower level of the building. Silence. Jones's tattoos pulsed. His ring throbbed. Magic.

"Olly olly oxen free," said Jones. "Come on out, Dutch Boy."

A tall figure stepped into view at the far end of the warehouse clapping its hands in mocking applause. "Very good, Wormwood." Behind him a man came carrying a lantern: Malone. In his other hand he held a leash attached to a harness around Frankie's shoulders. The boy looked dazed, in shock but alive.

The figure who spoke was dressed in a black suit with a matching silk hood over his head. "Jones—if that's what you choose to call yourself now. I should have known from the start that it would take one of Hennessey's boys to throw a wrench into my plans. C. O. Jones: Covert Operative. How clever."

"Actually," said Jones, "It stands for Carbon Monoxide, Hutz. Undetectable but no less deadly."

The hooded figure laughed. "I would have tried to bring you in with me, but I knew from what happened at *Tamno Mjesto* that you didn't have the balls for it."

"For what? Petty crime? Fight fixing? Extortion? Gambling? Murder?"

"Oh, you poor dumb son of a bitch. I saw how magic worked for our esteemed government and I thought, why not let it work for me? But to build a power base, you need money; money to buy books, artifacts, people. What you've seen up to now is all groundwork. This country owes me, Jones. It owes me big, and I plan to collect."

Hutz pulled off the silk hood and Jones saw his face. The left side had the same movie star looks Jones remembered from the war but the right was a mass of scar tissue, livid skin like a melting candle. "They took my face and gave me a purple heart and a lousy fifty dollar a month pension. What they should have done was shoot me instead, all of us, because they taught us too well. Like Frankenstein's monster, I'm back to turn on my maker. I'll bring this country to its knees."

Keep him talking, thought Jones. Give Danny and the others time to get into position. "One small town at a time, huh? Today Brownsville, tomorrow the world?"

"Do you know why I came here, Jones? Because of the people. There's a whole generation of immigrants here who have been kicked around and ground underfoot for decades. They're ripe for revolution. And now, thanks to the draft, they're combat trained. I promise them power, recompense and revenge. I speak their languages. They trust me."

"And you're going to raise an army from Pennsylvania to take on the whole U.S.?"

"Not just Pennsylvania, Jones, and not just any army." Hutz spoke a command in a guttural voice that made Jones's blood run cold. From around the corner, the man-thing that once was Tony Motsko shambled into the room. Jones shuddered in spite of himself.

"I see you remember *Tamno Mjesto*. What you saw as a horror and an abomination I saw as magnificence, genius. Our friend Mister Motsko is my first. I promised him greater strength, and as his muscles grew, his brain shrank. With an army of these, I will utterly destroy this country."

"All he needs is a number tattooed on his arm. You're as bad as the Nazis we killed, Hutz. But I'm not here to listen to your radical claptrap. I brought the statue. Give me the boy."

"Yes, the statue. I thought at first to simply bargain the boy to get it back, to establish an oracle like the one we destroyed in Munich. What a waste that was. But now that I've met this boy, I realize he is the greater treasure."

"But only if you have this." Jones drew the statue from his coat. "Without it his ability is marginal."

"That is so. But if you will not give me the statue, I will take it from you."
Hutz raised his hand and a ball of blue flame sparkled in his palm. He
thrust the hand forward and the ball flew at Jones and flared around him,
bathing him in light. Then it dissipated, leaving him unharmed. Granny
Maybelle's charm was working.

"We seem to be at an impasse, Hutz."

"You underestimate me, Jones. You have brought one chip to bargain. I
have two." Hutz spoke another guttural command and Motsko disappeared
around the corner. The sight showed the terror to Jones before Motsko
returned holding a struggling Ellie roughly by her arms. She screamed,
wild eyed, "Help me Jones!" and the monster clapped a distended hand
over her mouth.

Hutz put an arm around her shoulders and stroked her tenderly. "I'm
sure you wouldn't want any harm to come to this lovely young thing."
Hutz whipped his arm from Ellie's shoulders around her neck, pulling her
away from the Motsko-thing and put a pistol to her temple. "Now, Jones,
what choice will you make?"

Jones flicked his wrist and the automatic slid from his shirt sleeve. He
fired two shots, one at Hutz's gun hand and another at his forehead. The
bullets found their mark but simply stopped in mid air and fell to the
rough concrete floor. Hutz laughed. "Unlike you, when the war ended, I
didn't try to put magic behind me. I pursued it, and oh, the things I've
learned."

Hutz put his gun in the other hand and reached into his pocket. He
drew out an intricate bone carving that looked to be a complex of Celtic
braids. "The knot of Emer," said Hutz, "carved from human bone and
steeped in the blood of three enemies. It makes me proof against human
weapons, Jones." His left side smiled. "How gallant of you to try to save the
lady, but how foolish." He let go of Ellie's neck and instead of twisting away
from him, she wound herself around Hutz's body in a lascivious pose.

"Ellie!"

"You fool," she hissed. "I've been playing you all this time and you
never saw it. My man wasn't killed in the war." She laid her head on Hutz's
shoulder and looked at Jones from the bottoms of her eyes. "My Johnny
came marching home. You never sensed any magic on me because I was
pure as spring rain, but look what I have now." Ellie peeled down the
shoulder of her dress revealing a glowing rune freshly branded into her
flesh.

"My dear," said Hutz, "Please take care of our little friend while Malone readies the boat." She took the leash and pulled Frankie under her arm as Hutz put his own around her shoulder. "Quite a family portrait, wouldn't you say, Jones?" Malone disappeared down the stairs. Hutz laughed again, the sound a cruel and hollow echo in the building. "I don't need magic or barter to take what I want." He barked an order at Motsko and the man thing began shambling across the room toward Jones. "Remember *Tamno Mjesto*, Jones. No magic, just good old Nazi science. Magic can't help you against him." He turned to Ellie with that hideous half smile and said, "Watch my dear, and see the future."

The Sight showed Jones the grandiose gesture Hutz would make, the bone knot in his hand as the man-thing lumbered toward him.

At a flash of intuition, Jones fired one of the cast bullets into Hutz's palm. The Knot of Emer protected Hutz but couldn't protect itself. The enchanted metal shattered the carved bone and passed through Hutz's suddenly unprotected palm. Hutz shrieked in pain and shock. Jones aimed his gun at Hutz's head and Ellie dropped Frankie's leash and threw herself between them. Maybe she thought Jones wouldn't shoot if she was in the way. She was wrong and she was dead before she fell.

Hutz screamed in rage and crashed through a window. Jones heard a splash in the river below. "Frankie! Run! Hide!" Jones shouted and the boy, as if wakened from a trance, looked around him and ran for the door. In the meantime, Motsko had plodded deliberately across the room and Jones was almost within his reach.

Jones fired a round into Motsko's left knee then his right in hopes of slowing him down. Motsko's boxing past, however dim in his consciousness, still guided his instincts and while Jones was dealing with Hutz, the monster had moved between him and any immediate escape. Whatever intelligence Motsko may have once had was gone, and the eyes that glared from under his thick-scarred brow blazed with feral hatred. He swung a thick arm backhanded at Jones and Jones ducked under it and rolled away. Before he could scramble to his feet, Motsko picked up a gear three feet across and six inches thick, raising it as high as his muscle bound shoulders would allow.

The monster heaved the gear at Jones with a grunt and a two-handed push. Jones jumped up and twisted to the side, but the gear caught his shoulder with enough force to tumble him backward over a pile of scrap. Jones fired his last bullet into Motsko's face with little effect. Motsko's shuffling feet pushed the mound of jagged metal aside as if he were wading through a pile of leaves.

Jones grabbed a length of steel rod the size and thickness of a baseball bat and swung it at Motsko's head. The creature dropped one shoulder and the rod struck the other. To Jones it felt as if he were hitting a tree. Motsko swung a clawlike hand and the rod went flying across the room to land with a clang on the concrete.

Jones backed away as the huge hands swung methodically at him, backing him along the blank wall. Motsko was herding him into a corner as he strained to keep out of reach of those powerful hands. In desperation, Jones dove between Motsko's legs, but in an unexpected move, Motsko threw himself backward and fell on Jones, slamming him into the concrete and pounding the air from his lungs.

Motsko plucked Jones from the floor and pinned his arms in a deadly hug. The creature breathed a foul mix of rotting meat and chemicals into his face. Stars swam in Jones's head. Distantly he heard the sound of a motor. Black walls closed in on his brain.

Then Jones felt something cold and hard against his neck. There was a roar in Jones's ear and a flash and a chunk of Motsko's neck disappeared in a red cloud. It was Dodie. A ratcheting sound and another explosion from the shotgun over Jones's shoulder. Motsko's head tilted to the side. A third shot and it fell from his shoulders. The death grip relaxed, and Jones slumped to the floor.

"The boy," gasped Jones.

"He's safe. He's outside in your car."

Jones's ears rang, but not so much that he didn't hear the crack of rifle fire. Danny. He heaved himself to his feet. "Come on! They're getting away."

They ran down the rutted road along the river and came to an outcropping of rock that hung over the river like a cantilevered balcony. Jones saw the speedboat wavering crazily one way then another until it pulled into a dock near the barge works. A single figure climbed out and dragged itself onto the pier. Jones knew at once who it was. Danny had killed Malone but only injured Hutz. "Can you hear me, Jones?" Hutz shouted in a voice that Jones heard more inside his head than in his ears. "What happens next is all on you. 'Look upon my works, ye Mighty and despair!'"

Hutz raised his hands and began an incantation. He threw something Jones couldn't see into the river and the water began to roil, throwing dark ripples across the moon-silvered surface.

"Holy Christ," whispered Dodie.

What rose from the river was blacker than black, almost an absence of light. It stood nearly a hundred feet tall and looked like an onyx monument with smooth shining facets but bending and rippling like gelatin. The mass sprouted angular limbs that struck the water and threw towering waves crashing into the riverbanks. It stood still as if listening for a few seconds then began undulating toward the town.

"Pray, Dodie," said Jones, "because no god will listen to me."

Jones pulled the knot out of Granny Maybelle's charm bag.

The sound of wind began as a murmur and rose to a cyclone pitch. What looked like a white comet shot from the bag. It pierced the creature, in one side and out the other, wound its glittering tail around it and pierced it again and again like a blazing needle and thread. The black mass shuddered and heaved, then collapsed into itself like a great blob of oil and disappeared into the river.

Jones turned to see Hutz on the pier another ball of blue fire cradled in his good hand. "Live to fight another day, Jones," the voice in his head told him. "That was the unit's motto. I will. Too bad you won't." The Sight showed Jones the flaming blue orb flying at him, unprotected now that Granny Maybelle's charm was spent. As Hutz raised his arm to throw, the rifle cracked again and Hutz fell forward into the river taking the fireball with him. The water hissed and boiled for a moment then resumed its current as rivers will as if nothing had ever happened.

Jones turned to Dodie whose hands were over his face. "Is it over, Jones?" He said through his fingers.

"Yeah, Dodie, I think it's over. But if I were you, I wouldn't drink the water. Let's take Frankie home."

CHAPTER FORTY-EIGHT

Later that night in Snowdon Square, Skitch laid Frankie on the sofa in his office and covered him with his suit coat. "Jones, he said, "I can't thank you enough, and I can't pay you enough."

"We'll talk about that tomorrow or the next day, Skitch. For now," he gestured at the sleeping boy, "you have more important things to take care of."

Skitch handed him the statue. "Take this damned thing. Just get it away from us and away from this town. No more Frankie guessing numbers, Jones. No more magic."

"Without the statue nearby, Frankie should be just another normal happy kid." For now, thought Jones, at least for now.

Jones walked out the door of the poolroom, nodding to Danny and Dodie and climbed into his car. He was as tired as he had ever been in his life, but there was one last detail he had to manage. He drove the Ford down a country road parallel to the railroad tracks until he saw an orange glow in the sky ahead. He pulled his car to the side of the road and looked at the rank of coke ovens like squatting dragons belching fire and sulfur smoke. A gang of black men heaved shovels of coal into the ovens while others raked and stoked the fires.

Jones walked up behind the sweating men and one of them turned to him and said, "Who are you? You can't be down here, mister, it's dangerous."

Jones laughed and threw the statue into the glowing oven then watched as a blaze of sparks flew from the chimney like a swarm of glittering bees, swirled and vanished into the night. He took off the crude ring and held it in his palm for a moment then put it back on his finger. Without a word, Jones went back to his car and drove away.

CHAPTER FORTY-NINE

That night Jones dreamt he was walking through the woods to Granny Maybelle's house again. He came to the shanty town, but this time instead of menacing him, the people of the village circled around him and laid their hands on him, singing in a language he didn't recognize. As he watched, one by one his scars healed, and for the first time he could remember, he felt a sense of peace.

"Mister Jones. Granny Maybelle's waiting for you." Ephriam waited at the edge of the clearing. Where his mismatched eyes had once been two golden orbs glowed from behind his dark lids. He led Jones through the dense forest to the brick cottage where Granny Maybelle waited outside the door. Jones turned to speak to Ephriam but he had vanished.

"Ephriam—he's alive. I thought…"

Granny Maybelle smiled sadly, her face folding into its comfortable set of creases. "There is life, Mister Jones, and there is Life." She dabbed her eye with a threadbare handkerchief. "The bad thing is gone now. You are a truly good man, Mister Jones. It was noble to sacrifice your protection and put yourself at risk to save others. I believe that whatever circumstance brought you to Brownsville, it was part of the greater scheme of things. You were sent at this time to this place to serve where the need was greatest."

Granny Maybelle smiled again, this time beatific, and Jones reached out to touch her face, but stopped short when he heard a rasping sound nearby.

CHAPTER FIFTY

Jones woke suddenly to the scrape of the newspaper being shoved under his door. He sat up slowly, joints aching. He looked to the door and in the dim light saw that the headline was face up.

Instantly wide awake, Jones silently levered himself from the bed, listening. There were no footsteps in the hallway, no familiar clump of Marty's brace on the floor. Jones slipped his feet into his shoes and went to the window. No one was waiting on the fire escape and as far as he could see, no one was in the alley below either. He raised the sash and slipped out onto the sill, cocking the hammer of his automatic.

Jones leapt from the sill and landed with a clang on the fire escape. Through the window he saw two hitters outside his door. Before they could turn and shoot Jones fired through the pane and put at least three slugs into each one. He climbed into the hallway through the broken glass just as a man from a room down the hall yanked the door open. Jones fired a warning shot into the jamb that sent him scurrying back into his room. He kicked in the door of 307 and grabbed his coat and his valise. Jones hesitated for a moment then took the jar with Ephriam's eyes from the drawer and thrust it into his bag. They deserved a decent burial.

In a moment he was down the fire escape and running for his car. Nobody shot at him as he started the Ford and headed for the highway. Jones had recognized the killers, two of Benno Benaducci's men. Benno sent two this time. Next time he'd send more.

As Jones roared down Route 40 with the sun at his back, he thought again of his dream and wondered where the need would be greatest next.

THE END

ABOUT OUR CREATORS

AUTHOR -

FRED ADAMS - is a western Pennsylvania native who has enjoyed a lifelong love affair with horror, fantasy, and science fiction literature and films. He holds a Ph.D. in American Literature from Duquesne University and recently retired from teaching writing and literature in the English Department of Penn State University.

He has published over 50 short stories in amateur, and professional magazines as well as hundreds of news features as a staff writer and sportswriter for the now Pittsburgh Tribune-Review. In the 1970s Fred published the fanzine *Spoor* and its companion *The Spoor Anthology. Hitwolf, Six-Gun Terror* and *Dead Man's Melody* were his three first books for Airship 27 is his first, and his nonfiction book, *Edith Wharton's American Gothic: Gods, Ghosts, and Vampires* was published by Borgo Press in 2014.

INTERIOR ILLUSTRATOR –

CLAYTON HINKLE - is a life-long, self taught (for the most part) artist whose main ambition in life is to basically draw cool, adventurous, fantastic, horrorific Pulp and Comic art. Most, if not all, of his published work has been in the new Pulps of today, Airship 27 Productions being the major outlet of his wares by far, as well as work for the fanzine *REH, Two-Gun Raconteur*, a 'zine dedicated to the late, great Robert E. Howard and his works. He hopes to one day make his living by drawing, pure and simple.

COVER ARTIST -

CARL YONDER – growing up a military brat, he and his family traveled the country and eventually the world. His parents and artwork were the two biggest constants in his life. Over the years this love of art has developed into a passion he continues primarily with sequential art and painting. His work has been presented in foreign embassies, newspapers and other publications. He is currently illustrating the comic *Pirate Eye*: a hardboiled take on the high seas written by Josiah Grahn and published quarterly by Action Lab Comics. He has also completed several Fight Card covers. Carl can be reached at (www.carlyonder.com)

MORE FROM THE SAME AUTHOR:

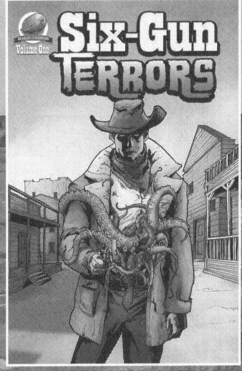

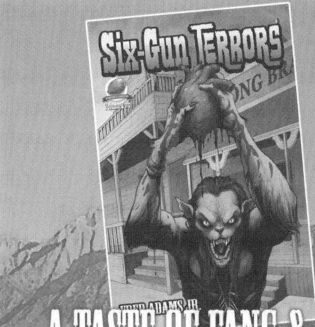

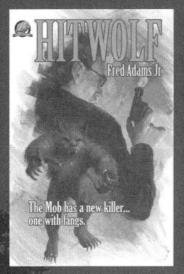